LILACS
FOR
JULIANA

By

Hearts Overcomi

DATE DUE

This book is a work of fiction. Any references to historical events, real people, or real places are used fictitiously. Other names, places, characters, and events are products of the author's imagination, and any resemblance to actual events or places or persons, living or dead, is entirely coincidental.

First Edition
August 2015

ISBN-13: 978-0692521571
ISBN-10: 0692521577

Cover Art by Cynthia Hickey
Photograph, of model Amber Goos, taken by Kathleen Harwell

Dedicated to
My Daughter
Cassandra Rose Pagels
My favorite baby girl.
Ever. And always.
And a blessing.

Introduction
The Christy Lumber Camp Series, Book Three

Readers of *The Fruitcake Challenge* and *The Lumberjack's Ball,* have already been introduced to my hero, Richard "Moose" Christy, and to my heroine, Juliana Beauchamps. Please bear with me, in the overlap with *The Lumberjacks' Ball*, Book Two. Book Three, *Lilacs for Juliana*, begins midway into the time frame of *The Lumberjacks' Ball*. One significant story element also occurs in *The Lumberjack's Ball*. However, I felt Juliana's and Richard's story had to start at their initial meeting.

I hope you will enjoy this next installment in The Christy Lumber Camp Series!

NOTE: The Beauchamps family chart follows, but the Author's Notes section, including historical information, is at the back of the book, as are acknowledgements, and information about the author and her other books.

The Beauchamps Family

Our heroine, Juliana Beauchamps, and her family:

Mrs. Eleanor "Nora" O'Rourke Beauchamps, almost 70 years old, matriarch, b. 1821. Bore last child at age 46.

Pierre Beauchamps, patriarch, b. 1819, *d. 1887.*

Gerard (also paternal grandfather's name), b. 1841, *died in Civil War 1863.*

Emmett (maternal grandfather's name, Emmett O'Rourke), b. 1843.

Pierre (also father's name) b., 1845, *d. 1865.*

Phillip (same as her uncle, father's eldest brother), b. 1846, *d. 1864.*

Sean (also her mother's eldest brother, Sean O'Rourke), b. 1854.

Pascal, b. 1857, *d. 1889*, m. to Melanie with 3 children.

Connor, b. 1859.

Juliana (named after the mother's mother, Juliana Lacy O'Rourke) Beauchamps, 28, b. 1863.

Claudette (named after her father's mother, Claudette Goullier Beauchamps), almost 24, b. 1867.

Carrie Fancett Pagels

Chapter 1

St. Ignace, Michigan - April, 1891

The scents of leather-bound volumes of Keats, Longfellow, and Wordsworth, the slightly acrid odor of ink, and the fresh aroma of paper enveloped Juliana. Seven years earlier, she'd finished her librarian studies and returned home to the brand new facilities and a job that she'd prayed for every night. She sighed contentedly, ready to begin her first children's reading group of the day.

Her assistant, Gracie, soon to age out of the orphanage at almost eighteen, waved at the twenty orphans being escorted in by Father Paul.

"Good morning, ladies." He smiled at them while clutching the youngest child's hand.

"Good day, Father." Juliana grabbed her book about life in the lumber camps.

Gracie inclined her head, with a hint of displeasure tugging at her pretty features.

Once they passed, Juliana touched the girl's shoulder. "It's not his fault, you know."

"I know, but where am I to go?"

"Like your priest and I have told you—God will provide. Plus, I feel pretty sure we can get you hired here." She hoped it wasn't wishful thinking.

Soon Juliana had joined the little group, read them a short nonfiction book, and engaged in one of her favorite pastimes—storytelling. While she loved reading, the oral tradition of telling tales had been passed down to her by both her Irish mother and her French father. One of his favorite stories was about Paul Bon Jean, and so she launched into an exciting story of Bon Jean clearing out all the pines in one Quebec town in only an afternoon.

Raising her hand high overhead, Juliana waggled her fingers. "So, the famous lumberjack, Paul Bon Jean, stood a head taller than any other man in the lumber camp."

Little Timmy Miller's blue eyes widened as he seemed to look past her.

After dropping her arm, Juliana pulled her lace shawl up over her head. She hunched over and rested her hand on Mr. Simmon's cane, borrowed for a prop. She warbled her voice, emulating her elderly Irish grandmother, "But Bon Jean possessed the kindest heart of all the shanty boys—regardless of what a huge man he was."

One of the most overactive of the children, Virginia, frantically raised her hand high but the others shushed her. *They must wish to hear the end of the story very badly to try to quiet that little firecracker.* Wobbling her way a few steps, Juliana scanned the group, who all now seemed to be focused on something, or someone, right behind her.

Oh no! Had that interfering library trustee come in yet again to observe her at work? She cringed.

One of the boys leaned forward and tugged at her scarf and pointed behind her. She'd not turn for anything—these kids were going to get the performance she'd promised them. "Not now, Timmy," she whispered to him.

"Bu...bu...but, Miss Juliana, Paul Bon Jean is here!"

Whirling around, Juliana almost tripped over the cane. She came face-to-flat belly with a giant's red-and-black-checked flannel shirt. She swallowed as a massive hand cupped her elbow, and steadied her. Taking a step backward, she spied red long johns peaking out at the top of the man's broad chest above his collar, where a tuft of dark chest hair was met by a shaggy black beard. As Juliana backed up one more step, her heel nudged against someone and a child squawked in protest. "Sorry!"

The giant Bon Jean lookalike cleared his throat. "Beggin' yer pardon, miss, but hearin' that story put me in mind of those we tell in the camps." His deep bass voice resonated through her.

From her viewpoint, Juliana could see the man's face, or what showed of it. Wavy dark hair protruded from beneath a faded red Frenchman's cap, met by equally dark eyebrows—ruler-straight over charcoal black eyes, which widened as he surveyed her from head to toe. Ivory skin shone around his eyes. His cheekbones and solid nose were kissed with rose-petal pink. *Kissed? Where had that word come from?* Maybe from those full, kissable lips easily viewed beneath his bushy beard. Juliana blinked, suddenly unsteady, and grateful for the giant lumberjack's grip on her person.

"Miss Beauchamps?" *No, no, a million times no.* The trustee supervisor entered the library, accompanied by two of his minions, both men clutching pads of paper.

She must have groaned aloud because Bon Jean's lookalike released her. "Are ya all right, Miss? Them fellas troublin' ya?"

Gaping at him, he must have read her expression because he swiveled to face the trio that surged toward them like Lake Michigan in its fury on a stormy day. "Good day, fellas."

Hatchens narrowed his eyes and craned his neck back. "We're with the library board."

"I'd say ya got a winner of a librarian here, ain't ya?"

When the trustee failed to respond, the lumberjack gestured toward the group of quiet children. "Sure makes me wish I was a little fella myself, again."

Tears of gratitude misted Juliana's eyes.

Somehow the lumberjack steered the men away from her. Juliana pressed a hand to her chest, her heart hammering against the stiffly starched fabric. "Let's get back to our story."

Timmy stood and handed her the cane. "But Miss Juliana, that was Paul Bon Jean."

Blonde curls bobbed vigorously on Virginia's fair head. "We want him to tell his story."

Unable to resist, Juliana swiveled around to view the titan again. Mr. Hatchens and his assistants had their backs to her as Bon Jean said something to them. His gaze connected with her and he winked. Heat burned her cheeks. The trustee and the minions turned, scowling as the stranger strode back over toward them.

"Look, he's coming." Edward Jennings, one of the older boys moved up to the front row and Juliana gestured him back—he was too tall and the others couldn't see.

Forcing herself to breathe, Juliana watched as Bon Jean pulled up a stout wooden chair, turned it around and straddled it, his muscular thighs bumping against her dark skirt.

Oh Lord, just let the floor swallow me up now. One of the tiniest orphans, Regina, stood and toddled up to Mr. Bon Jean. Goodness, she needed to discover his name.

"Bon Jean?" The dark-haired tyke pulled at his beard.

"Today I am." He grinned at the little girl. "Now, listen up and I'll tell you about my adventures."

A half hour later, Juliana still sat, her chin in her hand, transfixed. Surely her chair had become a wood stump and Bon Jean himself truly had visited with her sweet bevy of children, many of whom had begun life in the lumber camps.

"Ahem."

Juliana looked up into Mr. Hatchens' cold eyes. "Yes?"

He pulled his watch from his vest and tapped its face. "Time for our chat. And time for this little spectacle of yours to end."

Bon Jean stood and looked down at the man. "No disrespect, sir, but I'm simply a visitor and I'm guessin' this little gal needs to direct these children to their next activity. Right, Miss?"

She gave a curt nod. Saved again by the giant.

The door to the library opened and Sister Mary Lou, the pretty nun in charge of the orphanage, headed toward them.

"Good day, Mr. Hatchens. You must be telling the children about your plans to add a new playground to our field." She beamed at the man, whose face flushed red.

He leaned in. "That was supposed to be our secret, Sister."

"Oh! I'd forgotten." She shrugged dismissively and fluttered her hands at the children, who began to rise. "Thank you so much, Miss Beauchamps, for your program—our students love it."

"Not me today, Sister Mary Lou, but..." Juliana was going to point him out but Bon Jean seemed to have disappeared.

The trustee, too, left them and the tension eased in Juliana's neck.

Her friend leaned in. "He's good at causing pain, isn't he? I'll never figure that man out."

Juliana laughed.

"Say, when are you going to stop dressing like me, dear?" Sister Mary Lou frowned as she pointed out Juliana's black garments.

She sighed. "Makes me look more authoritative, don't you think?"

"The only thing it makes you look like is a tiny blackbird, my friend. The children have begun calling you the pretty little blackbird and that has to stop."

"What?" She couldn't help but scowl as several children giggled at this comment. "Why, I never..."

Bon Jean's dark head popped from behind a row of men's adventure books. He had the nerve to grin at her.

"We'll see you tomorrow then, Juliana?"

"I'll be here." If Hatchens hadn't fired her yet.

After Sister Mary Lou guided the children out of the library and presumably back to the orphanage, Juliana rejoined her assistant at the counter.

"Isn't he the prettiest trout in the stream?" Gracie sighed.

"Who?" Juliana quirked an eyebrow at the attractive girl. Who had caught her eye now?

"Mr. Christy, that's who." Gracie played with the silver chain on her slender neck and twisted the pearl dangling from it.

"Who is Mr. Christy?" The name had a nice ring to it.

"Bon Jean. Only he's really Mr. Christy the new lumber camp boss outside of town."

A camp boss. So he was more mature, as she'd thought, and not a green shanty boy. "How did you find out?"

"I asked him."

"You did?"

"Yes."

She'd have to try that herself next time.

"How?"

"He came up to the librarian station and asked about you and the children."

"He did?"

"Yes. Mr. Christy also checked out a pile of books." She fluffed her thick, curly hair. "He seemed much more interested in orphans and books than in me." Gracie picked up a fountain pen and made a curlicue C and then wrote out Christy on a patron card. "And he also spent a fair amount of time craning his neck to look at a certain dark-haired librarian."

Earlier in the day, when Richard had first entered the library, he'd planned to inquire about their collection of Mark Twain's work. The young helper, at the desk, said that if he wanted to check all of Twains' books out then he'd have to ask the head librarian, who was working with the children. Before he could get away, though, the pretty girl peppered him with more questions than a passel of camp cooks trying to find out who'd stolen a tray of biscuits. After answering a few of her inquiries, Richard had sought out the librarian. When he'd walked closer to where the children sat in a circle, he spied one of the older girls pretending to be an elderly woman. No sign of a librarian. Then he'd listened. The scarf on her head bobbed as she'd told the story of Bon Jean, one of the stories they loved sharing around the lumber camp, but she was doing it all wrong. Tiny, but with a commanding voice. And when she'd turned to face him, he'd changed his mind. That was no child, no crone, nor a librarian—that woman had the face of an angel framed by chestnut brown curls. Even at the recollection, his heart sped up as though he'd just cut down a mighty white pine.

Could be St. Ignace had some good things to offer. Sometime today he needed to stop at Cordelia Jeffries' inn and see if he might stay in town. The vacant lumber camp outside town, so isolated, was giving him the willies. Night sounds, usually so familiar in the woods, sounded eerie out there. He could admit that to himself, but danged if he'd tell his sister, Jo, who was busy with her new bakery. Maybe he'd share that with Ox—his brother would understand. Jo's future mother-in-law, Mrs. Jeffries', owned the inn and both she and Ox were already staying there. Their father remained with the lumber camp crew near Mackinaw City while Richard made arrangements for the new camp in the Upper Peninsula. Pa had placed a lot of confidence in him, allowing his youngest son to assume duties as camp boss while Ox pursued work as a carpenter and craftsman.

As part of his new duties, Richard had a lot to accomplish in St. Ignace before he headed back out to what would soon be his Christy Lumber Camp. He stopped at the largest newspaper and placed his ad for the cooks he'd need, if he expected to keep his shanty boys happy. He paid the clerk, who dipped his fountain pen in a nearby inkpot and recorded the transaction. "Say, can ya tell me which store is the best in town?"

"Labron's store is the biggest."

Probably one of their newspaper ad customers, too, which might be why the clerk recommended Labrons', but Richard would check it out. "Thanks. I think I passed it walking here."

The sandy-haired man jerked his thumb backwards. "Two blocks up."

After he'd entered through the mercantile's heavy walnut doors, Richard scanned the huge store for the register. A half-dozen men hovered around the counter, behind which stood a tall, ginger-haired man he assumed was the proprietor. The customers smoked pipes, some making purchases, and the others simply clutching newspapers. Some people had no sense. *With all this wood, any kind of smoking should be prohibited.* As a lumberjack, he knew to respect the power of fire.

"Excuse me, sir." The queue parted and he approached the counter. "I'm Richard Christy, the new Camp Boss outside of town at Grand Corners."

"Pleased to meet you." But the man's eyes flickered past him to the men behind. "I'm Charles Labron, the proprietor."

Labron was only a few inches shorter than him. Unexpectedly, that old sensation of being ready for a fight rose up in him. So many men had challenged him to a tussle over the years. But this mercantile owner held out his hand and didn't squeeze Richard's knuckles off when he shook his hand. Richard tried to push aside his jitters. How was he going to get the camp a reasonable food contract, and not get fleeced, if he came across as more fidgety than a green lumberjack with his first cut?

"Sir, I need the price to fill an order for victuals for one weeks' feed. It's for a camp of fifty to seventy five men."

Mr. Labron spit out a number. The cost quoted to him exceeded what he'd expected by about twenty percent, and Richard's head swam at the difference between what he'd anticipated and what was fact.

"Thank you." He turned, and the men again swarmed the counter.

"Yost? You say it was him?" The bank president, who Richard had met earlier, asked Labron.

"Yes, sir. The brewery owner himself."

"What's he doin' up here so early—when it's not even the season?" a beaver-coated man grouched.

Richard ran his hand through his hair, as an ache spread atop his head. Already he was failing. Should have known things would be more expensive above the straits.

A pretty blonde, in modest attire, pulled Richard aside, tugging at his wool sleeve. "Excuse me, I think my husband may have misquoted you back there, sir. I'm Mrs. Labron and I'd be glad to help you."

Hope sprang up. Even a five percent difference would help with overhead costs. "Ma'am?" He'd not thought to remove his Frenchman's cap, but pulled it off now and clutched it to his chest.

"My husband is a bit distracted because..." She stood up on tiptoe and cupped her hands around her mouth. He bent down to hear her whispered words. "James Yost, the famous beer baron from Milwaukee, was just here in our store!"

She straightened, her eyes bright.

"You don't say?" Not that Richard had heard of Yost. He didn't drink spirits, and truth be told, he'd rather read a novel than the newspaper. But his gaze suddenly settled on the large sign near the beer bottles, which clearly showed the man's name in huge fancy lettering. "I can see where having a man of such importance in his store might fluster Mr. Labron, ma'am."

Her cheeks flushed pink. "Oh my, and now I'm flustered, too—you must be Bon Jean!"

He stiffened then laughed. "You mean I was Bon Jean at the library. Did you get to watch?"

She motioned to a tawny haired boy. The youngster had been one of the boys sitting on the fringe of the group; well-dressed and obviously not an orphan. "Matthew, son, come over here."

"Ma'am, please don't embarrass him. My name is Richard Christy and I'm the new camp boss out near Grand Corners."

She ceased gesturing and her red-faced son scurried toward his father, who was animatedly gesturing to the beer display and his signs.

"He said you really surprised Juliana Beauchamps, the head librarian. She's a good friend of mine." She pulled a notepad from her apron and a short pencil. "Now let me see if I can help you out. Here's the quote for food for sixty men. Just realize that most of it will be tinned and we only have fresh during the season."

Taking the paper, he exhaled in relief. This figure was close to Pa's numbers from Mackinaw City. "Thank you, ma'am."

"Oh, and I'll include canned fruit with that when it is out of season. We possess a great many ladies in town who supply us with their jarred fruit. In fact, the Beauchamps provide those lovely preserves behind you." She pointed to a display of Mason jars filled with jams and jellies. "And they have recently inquired about providing baked goods to the camps, too."

"I'll have camp cooks for baked goods, ma'am, but I thank you kindly."

"Well, you haven't tasted a true northern cinnamon roll until you've had one of Mrs. Beauchamps'." Mrs. Labron had a pleasant voice with a musical quality to it. Richard could see where she'd be a wonderful help to her husband.

"Beauchamps a large family?"

"Oh yes, there are over a dozen." Mrs. Labron's features suddenly bunched. "That is, there were, but now just the three women still live here."

By themselves? Was the woman widowed? She must be. He needed to change the topic. "Well, I sure hope we'll see some of those jellies in our orders."

"Oh, I have no doubt that you'll have all you need." She chuckled and gave him a sly smile.

What was that supposed to mean? Women—who could figure them out?

Labrons' male patrons clustered in a circle outside the store, smoking and chattering animatedly when Juliana had entered. The men were probably chased out when her friend caught them puffing away inside the mercantile. Juliana fled the smoke and the chill breeze from the lake and hurried into her friend's store where she soon found Janet straightening a display of women's nightgowns. Janet Labron never looked a day older, whereas Juliana…Well, she didn't want to think about how her dark clothing accentuated the circles under her eyes. Her black and navy blue clothing conveyed that she was a professional woman with authority and not a child, like some early patrons had thought when she'd come to work attired in pastel dresses.

"I need some fabulous cloth—something sumptuous, like a light velvet or a heavy satin. Do you have new material in stock for the summer residents, but suitable for me?" Her words tripped over themselves. This would be her first time attending the Lumberjacks' Ball and she wanted to look perfect. Now to get Bon Jean, rather Richard Christy, to ask her.

Janet blew out a puff of breath. "I'm so sorry, Juliana—but we haven't gotten our newest shipment of fabrics in yet. We're not gearing up for the Lumberjacks' Ball, or the tourists, until another month."

Her old friend likely didn't remember how long it took for a dress to be made. Janet had both the luxury of being an average size woman and the ability to choose whatever ready-to-wear items she wished to have. "I don't have much time to myself for stitching, much less looking…"

Janet hooked her arm through Juliana's and pulled her toward the display of threads, buttons, and lace. "Matthew came home from the library all excited because he said you'd invited Bon Jean to come speak. Tell me all about it."

Stepping back, Juliana waved her friend away. "I don't need rumors started."

The pretty store proprietress frowned. "About what?"

She chewed the inside of her lower lip. "Nothing."

"A mysterious stranger—and you need a new dress for the Lumberjacks' Ball." Janet clasped her hands together, her long blonde braid bouncing on her shoulder. "Sounds interesting."

"Shhh!" Juliana eyed the other customers—Mrs. Pickleman picking out tinned goods, Mr. Nelson chatting with Mr. Labron, and Gertrude Parker gently touching a baptismal gown.

"Is that old Hatchens really trying to add a requirement that the librarians not marry?"

"What?"

"That's what Charles told me. He attended the board meeting last night."

Juliana ground her teeth together.

"Don't worry—he's just a windbag."

"Charles or Mr. Hatchens?"

Janet playfully slapped at Juliana's shoulder. "Oh, you."

"Well, I better go." No need staying and hearing any more unpleasant news.

"Come back in a couple of weeks for the new fabric."

It would be too late then. "We'll see."

"I agree you need something new." Janet grinned. "It's about time you ceased this silly habit of dressing entirely in black. You remind me of a little blackbird, or worse yet, a crow."

"A crow?" Juliana feigned offense but couldn't help laughing. "Caw! Caw!" She opened her black wool-covered arms and waved her black rectangular pocket book. She stomped her heavy leather boots. First Sister Mary Lou and now Janet—both of her friends trying to reform her.

Laughing, Janet leaned in. "Trust me, you'll not put any fear in the heart of Hatchens with that performance."

"Oh, pooh. I suspect you're right." So much for thinking the dark clothes made her appear more formidable.

"You better go. He's probably down there shivering by the library's back door, waiting your inevitable late return."

"Probably."

Janet raised her index finger. "But before the fair librarian departs, methinks she must hear of the town square news."

"Oh?" The men were obviously enthused about something.

"Who do you want to hear about—the beer baron or Bon Jean?"

Her hands began to tremble and she clutched her purse tighter. "As I don't know any beer barons, I'll pick the latter."

"Good choice!" Dimples formed in Janet's pretty face. "First of all, his name is Richard Christy."

Juliana nodded. She knew that. She resisted looking up at the clock. "Yes?"

"And I believe he'll be buying all his tinned and canned goods from us." Janet clapped her hands together.

"Excellent."

"Also, I believe he's anticipating tasting some of the wonderful Beauchamps jellies and jams we offer here." She giggled, and from that sly look, Juliana knew her friend had done or said something.

"What did you do?"

"Me? Nothing. But he was very interested when I pointed them out to him."

She sighed. "As are most men—they all have stomachs, don't they?"

Janet waggled her eyebrows. "But how many men stare at the local librarian like she's the jam?"

"Janet Labron!" Beyond them Mrs. Parker glared. Had she heard? Or was she over there thinking of something snide she might say to Juliana about Aleksanteri? He'd been the former-teacher's favorite pupil.

Thankfully, Mrs. Parker moved away from them, toward the cast iron skillets.

Janet leaned in. "Matthew said he looked like he could just eat you right up with a spoon."

"He did not!"

She shrugged. "No, but he did say he was watching you the whole time."

Juliana shook her head but she hoped it was true—and that soon she'd be the belle of the ball at the dance.

After they hugged, Juliana headed toward the door, trying to resist the lure of the peppermint sticks. The children loved them so much. When she broke the candy into tiny pieces there always seemed enough to go around—like the fishes and the loaves.

Janet had returned to the sewing notions, and from the counter, Charles motioned her over. He was ringing up Mr. Gustafson's purchases of sardines, rye crackers, and a jar of Momma's spiced apples, which appeared to be the railroadman's lunch. Juliana was glad she had her own ham sandwich waiting for her to eat before she went back on the clock.

"You're not leaving without these, are you?" He reached beneath the sturdy oak counter and brought up a paper bag and handed it to her. "I heard what you've been doing with all those sweets you buy."

She peered inside the hefty bag. "Thank you." At least a dozen of the long sticks filled the satchel. "God bless you, Charles, you're a good man."

He jerked a thumb toward his wife. "Just keep telling her that, all right?"

She laughed and headed out to the street, a gust of cold air blasting her face—the one unprotected part on her body. Juliana pulled her ebony scarf up around her cheeks, the knit garment nearly the same color as Mr. Christy's dark eyes. She drew in a frosty breath and marched on.

Carefully, she avoided the icy spots on the walkway and made her way down the street to the new mercantile. They had very little merchandise but just maybe… As she opened the heavy door to the town's newest store, she was greeted by the scent of varnish and new wood. She spied a severely dressed young woman unrolling a bolt of dusky pink-red moiré satin, the end draped over her shoulder. The fabric was perfection. She watched as the woman rolled it back up. Maybe she should wait for Janet to get her stock, but this was so beautiful.

Making a decision, she stepped forward. "Could I...that is...the fabric you just put up—is it claimed?" Her boot heels clicked across the wood floor as she joined the woman at the counter and removed her gloves. She gently touched the raspberry-colored fabric. "It's so pretty. And I need a new gown made up for me. They don't have anything like this at Labrons."

"Take off your hat." This must be Rebecca Hart, the new proprietress, who smiled and pointed to the nearby wooden rack. "Let's see how this color goes with your hair."

"Oh." She patted the unruly dark curls framing her face and then removed her cap. "I'm afraid I usually pin my hair up, so you won't see it well."

But wouldn't Bon Jean, or rather Mr. Christy, like to see her hair down? The store owner had a lovely face but with her hair pulled back so tightly and her clothes so drab, she reminded Juliana of a dove. What was the pensive woman mourning?

"I'm wanting a new dress for the Lumberjacks' Ball."

"Oh, yes, I've heard about that. So you've already been invited?"

Heat seared her cheeks. Miss Hart was certainly direct. But it had been Juliana's experience that such women were often more trustworthy. "Not yet, but I'm praying Mr. Christy will invite me."

"Mr. Christy?" Miss Hart blinked rapidly. "Oh, I see. Well, he's a very nice man."

"I know." She smiled, remembering his kindness to the children. "I'm Juliana Beauchamps, the librarian."

"Oh. Nice to meet you, Juliana. I'm Rebecca Hart, the proprietress of this mercantile." A frown worked between the woman's brows. What troubled her?

"You should come down to the library and get signed in as a patron. We have many good titles, despite our location."

One of the orphans, Amelia, entered, and Juliana gave her a tiny wave. "Morning! How are you doing today?" She bobbed a curtsey. After Amelia had hung her coat up, she returned and unrolled the rosy satin and stretched it over Juliana's shoulders. "Doesn't this color look lovely on Miss Beauchamps?"

The proprietress seemed to have lost her tongue. What on earth was the matter with Miss Hart?

"Rebecca, are you all right?" Might as well be as direct with the woman as she was with her.

"Yes." She offered a tight smile. "Have you met Amelia? She's my new helper."

"Indeed, the children from the orphanage come regularly to pick out the books they wish to read. And Amy likes Louisa May Alcott's books best, don't you?"

"Yes, ma'am."

"And the fashion books, too. Am I right?" Juliana smiled at the girl, who would soon be her own height.

Together, they examined all the new fabrics, oohing and aahing over the lovely selection.

Amelia suddenly touched Juliana's upswept hair. "I bet your hair is as pretty as my mother's if you'd let it down and curl it."

In a flash, the orphan removed two large pins, and Juliana's hair fell to her waist in a mass of curls. Oh no, now she'd have to put it back up and she'd be even later.

A burst of frigid air entered the establishment and with it came a broad-shouldered man, whose gaze fixed determinedly on Miss Hart. He was almost as handsome as Bon Jean.

"Good morning, ladies."

"Good day, Mr. Christy." Miss Hart's harsh tone suggested it was anything but a good day.

So here was another Christy. She took him in. Yes. Same dark hair and eyes, but this man was perhaps a half foot shorter maybe less. Bon Jean seemed to fill up the room. But this man looked like he could wrestle a black bear and win. "Mr. *Christy*? Are you related to the *other* Mr. Christy?" With his smooth cheeks and unlined complexion he must be the younger brother.

She stretched up on tiptoe and held her hands high. "Even taller than you?"

He removed his coat and hung it next to Amelia's.

"Yes, ma'am, I'm his..." His low voice rumbled, obscuring his next few words, then said, "brother."

Rebecca frowned.

Juliana cocked her head, unsure of what his mumbled word meant—but by the way he smiled and Amelia laughed, it was supposed to be funny.

"Just a joke." He mumbled something that sounded like, "my brother."

"He's here, too?" Miss Hart's voice came out a whisper.

Juliana almost sighed aloud, thinking about how Bon Jean, or rather Mr. Christy, this man's elder brother, had entertained the children. Anyone who cared about orphans like he did must have a huge heart to match his height. For the first time since Aleksanteri had abandoned her, she found herself wanting to spend time with a man. How she'd missed dancing. She had to get him to ask her to the Lumberjacks' Ball. "I met him at the library just this morning." Oh heavens—only this morning? Had she lost her mind? *Or heart? And so quickly!*

"This morning?" Both he and Rebecca uttered the words simultaneously.

Did they know what she was thinking? About how handsome and kind the older brother, Richard, was? She had to get going. She tugged at her collar. "Yes, well, I really have to get back to the library. I just wanted to look at some fabric for a dress."

"She's making a dress for—"

"Amelia!" Rebecca thankfully interrupted the child's sentence.

Juliana held her breath.

In a moment, Miss Hart accompanied Richard's younger brother to the back, where he was to work on some cabinets. It seemed rather sad that his brother was setting up camp all by himself and hadn't even asked his younger one to help. Perhaps Bon Jean wasn't as fond of family as she'd hoped. She'd find out. Because he would take her to the ball, one way or another. He had to—or her head and her heart wouldn't give her any peace.

What about God, a tiny voice nagged. Juliana gritted her teeth. She still attended church. She still said her prayers. And she still believed. Wasn't that enough? Why should she consult God about romance? Look what had happened with Alek—the man she thought God wanted her to wed.

Chapter 2

If his brother, Moose, hadn't custom-made him a tall dining chair, Richard would be seated on a chaise—with his knees practically hitting his chest. But they'd hauled the big oak chair into the fancy wallpapered parlor in the inn that morning so Richard could interview camp cook applicants.

A squat woman with beady dark eyes sat across from him. "I can't believe you're asking for a reference for a camp cook job." She pursed her lips.

"Yes'm, seems to me that shouldn't be too hard with yer good cookin' here." He took a bite of a peanut butter cookie that she'd brought, careful not to chip a tooth on the stale thing. Good thing he gave her the compliment before he took a bite of the thing she passed off as a cookie. It had looked good. But he wouldn't want to lie. He had no intention of hiring her and needed to wrap this talk up.

"You're a smart man and exactly right, Mr. Christy—my bakery goods speak for themselves."

"Yes'm, they sure do." He rose and indicated for her to do the same. "Do ya mind sendin' the next lady in?"

"Do I have the job?" Her shrill voice made him clench his teeth.

"I'll decide after I've finished talkin' with all the ladies, ma'am."

She harrumphed and headed out of the parlor, straight past the bench on which several other women perched. Richard exhaled and strode out to call in the next applicant. He had to hire an excellent crew as he was down three cooks, all of them known as being the best in the camps downstate.

He had a reputation to keep up for the Christy Lumber Camp if he wanted to keep his lumberjacks up above the straits of Mackinac.

When he had finally finished, Cordelia stepped into the parlor. She looked at him almost a full minute before they both started to laugh. "That was quite an interesting group, wasn't it?"

"Never seen anything like it, Miss Cordelia." He scratched his cheek, beneath his beard. "Right unusual clothing they wore."

She raised one eyebrow at him. "Well, let's have some lunch and make a new plan."

The front door to the inn opened and then groaned shut. Within a minute, the sheriff entered. "What did you think of my ladies? Glad I let them out?"

"What?" Richard barked out the words and the lawman raised a hand.

"Just trying to help out. Heard you needed help and those women could use another profession."

"Sheriff Edwards," Cordelia stomped a foot. "Are you telling me you sent women of ill repute into my inn?"

"No, I never said that." The man grinned.

Richard shook his head. "If it keeps on goin' like this I reckon I'll have to run over to Newberry and see who I can find there."

Cordelia continued to glare at Edwards.

"I'm thinkin' yer not gonna get a lunch invite today, Sheriff." Richard tore his notes in half and was about to toss them in the waste bin when Cordelia took them from him.

"I came here to ask if you had noticed anything unusual out near your camp, Richard."

Prickles raced up his spine. "Not sure, but somethin' ain't right out there."

"Seen anything of your neighbor?"

"Nope, he seems to be keepin' to his cabin."

"Mrs. Beauchamps says she's had some of her eggs stolen recently but it could be animals getting in. Don't say anything to that librarian friend of yours, though, because her mother is keeping that under her hat for now—says Juliana has enough to concern herself with."

Such as? He wanted to ask, but refrained. "I've heard and seen deer and an occasional bobcat, and there's been something…" or was it someone? "…in the woods at night."

Cordelia took his arm. "Please stay in town with us until more of the camp moves up."

"Might be a good idea if you keep to town for now." The sheriff waggled his eyebrows. "Rumor has it you're a regular patron at our library. I'm sure Miss Juliana wouldn't object, either."

Heat crept up Richard's neck. He dare not say anything smart back to the sheriff so he held his tongue. Yes, he had gone to the library every time he was in town and always he'd talked with Juliana, and she'd taken his focus off finding the help he needed for the new lumber camp.

Sheriff Edwards tipped his hat. "Good day."

Cordelia followed the man out into the hallway, waving her hand before her face. "Goodness that cheap perfume stinks."

The lawman laughed. "Thought you wanted more folks coming to the inn, Cordelia."

As he exited the front door, she called after him, "Goodbye, Sheriff, and please don't continue that type of favor—we don't need it."

Richard stood and stretched to his full height, admiring the coffered ceiling overhead.

Ox strode in from the back, carrying with him the scent of turpentine and wood. "Quite the little parade ya had today, brother."

The inn owner splayed her hand outward. "Don't even start with him. It's all the sheriff's fault."

Ox shrugged. "Rebecca made you a new sign to advertise for camp cooks, with bigger letters, and put it in her front window."

"Please tell her thanks for me." Ox was clearly smitten with Rebecca Jane but Richard withheld a teasing comment.

"Young man, you shall convey that message yourself, as you shall be staying right here." Hard to believe this handsome woman would soon be his sister's mother-in-law, when Jo married Tom Jeffries.

Ox chuckled. "My little brother is gonna be camp boss soon, Mrs. Jeffries. I can't wait for ya to talk to him like that in front of a lumberjack crew."

"No different than Ma did." Richard sighed. "And, yes ma'am, I'll thank Rebecca proper-like when I see her."

After lunch with Cordelia and Ox, Richard headed to the library. This time he would get a book and not be distracted by a pair of big blue eyes. Heck, the way the sheriff acted, ya'd think he only went there to take a gander at Juliana Beauchamps. Knowing which book he wanted, Richard went straight to the shelf and tucked a copy of Horatio Alger's *Ragged Dick* under his arm and headed toward the librarian's desk. He let out a little whoosh of air when Gracie, the assistant, grinned at him—Miss Beauchamps was nowhere in sight. Although he should be relieved, loneliness tugged at him. He strode forward and slid his book onto the counter just as a dark head bobbed up from behind the counter.

"Oh, Mr. Christy, so good to see you!" Her breathy voice seemed to suck the air from the room. He froze.

"You, too." He needed to get outta there right quick. He shouldn't have come here. He should have gone to all the newspapers and put new ads in them. No time for a lady friend to distract him from his mission, which was to get Pa's new lumber camp set up. No—not Pa's—*his* new lumber camp.

The dark topknot on Miss Beauchamps head bobbed up and down—was she bouncing on her toes? She must be. From the advantage of his height he peered over and sure enough, she was.

He straightened. Who was he fooling? If he wanted to place those ads he'd have gone right after lunch instead of over here to the library. What was he going to do about his fascination with this perky little lady?

"Isn't the weather improving?" The librarian blinked up at him.

"Yes'm. I 'spect it'll be right pretty for Easter Sunday."

"Oh, I do love Easter. It means the lilacs will soon be in bloom."

Easter. Lilacs? He'd never made the association. Weren't that many downstate in the last town. "There many of them kinda flowers up here?" They made him ill.

"Oh, yes. The French brought them here centuries ago."

As was he, but how that related to anything he didn't know. His mouth went dry. "Um, yes'm, if ya say so."

"And as you can probably tell, I'm of French descent." Again, she blinked up at him, those dark blue eyes contrasting with her pale skin and thick, dark hair. Why she was more lovely than any flower he'd ever seen? "And I'm Irish, too."

"Me, too—Irish that is. Maybe French, too. Don't rightly know." He scratched his head.

She scanned the cluttered desk before her. "Now where is my fountain pen?"

He pointed to it, right in front of her, and she blushed, making her look even lovelier. "Are you looking forward to Spring, Mr. Christy?"

"Yes'm, I'm looking forward to going to church on Easter." Now why had he said that? Of course he was. For once he'd be able to sit in a pew instead of on a stump or in the cook shack as a borrowed parson spoke to the lumberjacks.

Would he need new clothing? Shucks, that was one more expense he'd have to enter in the ledger. Didn't need his older sister Jo yelling at him. What clothes could he wear?

"Ahem."

Miss Beauchamps held the nib of her fountain pen over her cut glass inkwell and gazed expectantly at him. Her eyes widened and she beamed up at him. What had he said? "Should I record your borrow of this notable children's book, Mr. Bon Jean?"

He blinked at her. "I ain't Bon Jean." She didn't have to point out that it was a children's book he borrowed.

Her lips pulled into an adorable pouty smile, flummoxing him further. "I was just teasing—I know your name is Mr. Richard Christy, but I was hoping you might like to share some excerpts from the book as Bon Jean. Would you come again for the orphan's reading group today?"

Before he could reply, Mr. Hatchens appeared from behind a nearby row of books, the nonfiction section devoted to business. "Miss Beauchamps!"

The little lady jumped nearly a foot off the ground and Richard fixed the man with a gaze that he hoped would reflect his aggravation at the interruption.

"Here you go, Mr. Christy." The librarian gave him a curt nod and crooked her finger at the lady behind him, who clutched a stack of books to her chest.

"Sorry, ma'am," he said to the woman as he turned to leave. "Woulda gotten out of your way, if I'd known you were there."

"It's all right. I was young once, too." She gave him a motherly smile which should have warmed him, but instead sent a pain through his heart.

"Yes'm. You have a nice afternoon." What would Ma have said if she'd found him loitering at the library when he should be setting up the new camp?

He turned to leave, but catching Hatchens glaring at Miss Beauchamps, Richard pointed to the sign behind him and spoke to the interfering trustee. "Sir, I reckon ya might not know, but only employees of the library are allowed back there."

"I'll have you know…" Hatchens' beady eyes narrowed behind his wire-rimmed eyeglasses.

Richard raised his hand. "Yeah, yer a board member, but ya ain't an employee, are ya? So git on out of there before I offer ya an escort."

Behind him someone laughed but Richard kept focused on the trustee.

"How dare you lecture me, when you are up here distracting this employee?" As Hatchens' jabbed a finger at Richard, spittle flecked the ornery man's cheeks.

Grabbing the man's index finger, Richard pressed it down to the counter and leaned in until they were almost eye-to-eye. "Mr. Hatchens, I'm a patient man. Let me explain once for ya. I…borrowed…a children's…book…which I intend to read to the orphans in this library for a trustee-approved program. So I had legitimate business talking with the librarian—unlike you." That wasn't exactly true two minutes ago, but it was now.

The chuckle stopped and someone tapped Richard on the shoulder. A well-dressed gent winked at him and stepped past him to the counter and extended his hand to the trustee. "Mr. Hatchens, I'm James Yost, a library board member in Milwaukee, and I believe this young man is correct—even trustees are not allowed in the librarian's domain during work hours. Not unless the board has tasked him to do so. And as I attended last night's board meeting, I know they did not."

Hatchens' face turned a mottled shade of purple and Richard expected him to begin spitting nails.

The wealthy beer baron stood straight and proud, awaiting a reply.

So this was James Yost. He wasn't much older than Ox, maybe thirty or so. And he looked like he'd just stepped out of a fine haberdashery. Reminded Richard of one of the lumber tycoons he'd met with his Pa—a bad man who stole, cheated, and encouraged his shanty boys to take up with prostitutes, even going so far as to cart them into the camps after payday. Richard shuddered. Marvin Peevey had gone off to work in such a place and look what happened to him—almost killing Janie and then going to prison. This fellow, Yost, looked pleasant, though, and rumors in town claimed he was a donor to many charities in Wisconsin. Shouldn't judge a man simply by his appearance—that worked both ways for the shabbily dressed and those all turned out well, like the wealthy man was.

Clenching his fists, Hatchens glared at the beer baron and then at Richard. "Well, I never…"

Shrugging, Richard tucked the Alger book under his arm.

Yost gestured to Richard. "Furthermore, as this gentleman has pointed out, when patrons are volunteering, do you truly wish to have your fair librarian drive them away?" The man's voice took on a dreamy quality, which was probably supposed to soothe the trustee, but had the effect of setting Richard's teeth on edge. Who was Yost, a stranger, to be commenting on Miss Beauchamps' appearance?

A smile tugged at Miss Beauchamps' mouth as she recorded the next patron's borrows. Had she heard Yost? Was she flattered? A muscle in his cheek jumped. Who was he to be concerning himself with what Yost had to say to this pretty little librarian? Heck, why would she ever want to associate with a gargantuan who would make her look even tinier than she was? But she sure didn't seem intimidated by his size. Juliana Beauchamps had spunk. And that gave him hope.

Juliana hurried into Miss Hart's shop, greeted her, and then shared her wonderful news. At least she surmised it was good news and that an invitation had indeed been extended, albeit obliquely. She'd run this by Miss Hart, whose directness should help her clarify. "I just saw my Mr. Christy, again."

"You did?"

"Yes, and I think he's invited me to attend Easter service with him." She inhaled deeply, catching the scent of sawdust, which still dusted the floor.

"Oh."

"At least I think he asked me. He stopped by the library to get a book. Then he said he was looking forward to going to church on Easter. Then he gazed right at me for what seemed like a full minute."

"And what did you say to him?"

"I couldn't say anything, my supervisor came up and librarians are not allowed to be having private conversations with the clients." She'd not tell her how Richard stood up for her. That was something that tonight, in the privacy of her bedchamber, she'd relive in detail. "Particularly not single librarians and unmarried, young men."

Rebecca's facial muscles tugged as though she wanted to say something but couldn't.

Easter was coming soon. "So now I need to have my dress made up sooner. I need something really special."

"I hear Labrons' Store has a good selection."

That's where Juliana should have gone during her break. After all, Janet had told her that her new fabrics would be coming in. And they'd begun carrying some ready-to-wear clothing, too, but most was sized for someone of average height, even though Juliana had complained to her friend to acquire some shorter garments for her store.

One of her most attentive library patrons, Amelia, joined Rebecca and Juliana. "Might I go to the library, Miss Beauchamps?"

"If Miss Hart agrees." Juliana brushed a stray curl from the girl's forehead. Poor thing had lost her parents and was now separated from her siblings, who remained at the orphanage on Mackinac Island.

A smile tugged at Rebecca's lips. "Certainly."

"And I'll ask at Labrons', but I'm afraid I don't have a lot of hope of finding one for my height."

"I understand. And we can make arrangements to order some ready-to-wear that just might fit. I know a supplier from Detroit who used to send us some at my father's shop in lower Michigan."

"Wonderful!" Juliana departed feeling that a new beginning might be just around the corner.

When Juliana and Amelia stepped out of the building, both shivered and leaned in toward each other as a chill breeze blew in off the lake, threatening to chase her happy disposition. Across the street, railroad cars slowly rumbled out across the tracks. Overhead, huge puffs of white clouds dotted the azure sky. They stepped carefully over icy spots on the walkway. "I have some good news for you—Bon Jean is supposed to read this afternoon."

"Bon Jean?" Amelia frowned then a grin split her tiny face. "Ah, you mean *your* Mr. Christy."

Juliana froze in her tracks. Hearing the child use her own words, hearing her put it that way, sounded frighteningly silly of her. "Well, he's not exactly my Mr. Christy." Not yet.

"I know. But it sounded nice to say." She laughed, not in a mean way like some of the girls at school used to do, but in a sweet way.

"I like Mr. Richard a lot, too."

"You do?"

"Yes." She slipped her bare hands into her shabby coat pocket. Juliana would check and see if she had an outgrown coat that might fit the child.

"Have you seen much of him?"

"Mr. Christy came to the orphanage and asked Sister Mary Lou how many children were there and how many boys and girls and their ages."

"I see." But she didn't.

"He's buying us all gloves—Mrs. Labron gave him a huge discount."

Her heart gave a little thud beneath her heavy coat. "That is so sweet."

"Sister Mary Lou says he's a kind-hearted man, but I think he's just got a great big heart because he's so tall. What do you think?" Amelia began to giggle.

Juliana pretended to hit at the bright little girl's shoulder. "Does that mean I have a small heart then?"

"I'll have to research that at the library, Miss Beauchamps."

Laughing, the scent of fresh-baked cinnamon bread drew her to the new bakery. Miss Josephine Christy's place. "Say, do you mind if we stop by here for a minute?"

Amelia wasn't much shorter than Juliana was and the orphan's shoulder bumped into her arm. The child gazed up at her with wide eyes. "Can we?"

Feeling in her pocket, Juliana discerned she had at least two bits, unless her gloved hands deceived her. "Yes, and we'll share a cookie, but don't tell anyone."

"Oh, I won't. I love good secrets. It's only the bad ones we need to tell—that's what Sister Mary Lou says."

Wouldn't that be wonderful if she could buy one cookie for each child instead of breaking peppermint sticks into bite size pieces? But she had others to think of. Reality knocked at her door. But she wasn't going to answer. Not when she could daydream all afternoon about sitting in the church pew with the Christy family.

Leaning in, Juliana whispered, "Maybe you can ask Miss Christy if she thinks Richard is kind-hearted."

She'd just reached out to open the door when she spied the customer at the counter—Mr. Hatchens. And the clock behind Josephine Christy showed that Juliana was going to be fifteen minutes late getting back to the library. Pulling Amelia quickly past the building, she bit her lip.

"But Miss Beauchamps…"

"I have to get back to work. I'm late. I'm so sorry." She'd be even sorrier if the trustee found out she was on an extended break. She reached into her pocket and retrieved the coin for Amelia. "You stop by on your way back to the mercantile and get yourself and Miss Hart a cookie, all right?"

Chapter 3

Despite Cordelia's insistence, after a few days, Richard had to return to the camp. He had work to accomplish and finally had one assistant who'd come out to work on repairs.

"Mrs. Beauchamps told me you might need help. I'm Avery Bell and I'm a handyman and jack of all trades." The man had told him when he showed up in camp that morning.

"She's right. I do." After the debacle with the cook interviews, Richard was skeptical. "How do you know the Beauchamps?"

"Well, I was in the same unit as her eldest son, Gerard, during the war." The man looked to be in his late forties. Did Juliana have a brother that old? Didn't sound right.

"Where is he now?"

Salt and pepper eyebrows drew together. "Buried in Virginia along with two of his younger brothers—only one came home."

He should have thought first before asking. "I'm sorry." Poor Juliana. She must have been a young girl then if what this fella said was true. Probably not even born yet. Easy enough to discover if this was true.

"I check in on Mrs. Beauchamps about once a week. She lives just yonder by the lake." He removed his slouch hat and gestured south. "Out of all those seven sons she bore, only one lives nearby and he's a fisherman. With a habit, if you know what I mean." He gestured as though drinking from a bottle. "Emmett keeps to himself."

Might be worth a try to hire this fella. Garrett extended a hand.

The two of them tackled the single men's building first, which needed a lot of work.

Later that afternoon, Sheriff Edwards rode out. He confirmed that Avery Bell had indeed served with the Michigan militia and the Beauchamps brothers. And so Bell had come on board as the first new employee at Christy Lumber Camp at Grand Crossing.

They'd worked hard all day but the sun was sinking lower over the treetops. A chill wind kept the newly-leaved trees swaying.

"We done for the day, boss?" Avery Bell was a good worker.

Richard nodded as he glanced around the bunkhouse, now much closer to being safe and sound with their repairs. "We've gotten a lot of work done today despite the cold weather."

The wiry man grinned and stuck a plug of tobacco in his cheek.

Daytime in the camp didn't bother Richard so much but soon it would be night. "Reckon yer wife might like to feed ya some dinner."

"You want me back tomorrow?"

"Sure thing."

"You got shotguns and all out here, too, eh?"

Richard was a grown man and shouldn't be afraid, but he wasn't stupid enough to think he didn't need weapons at the ready. "I do."

Between his older brother, Garrett's, and Mrs. Jeffries' encouragement, he knew moving into town was probably the wisest thing to do.

"Having survived the war, I can fend for myself, too, Mr. Christy, but I'm not sure I'd want to—if you get my drift. Might want to get some of your jacks who are willing to get themselves on up here soon."

"None so far and both my Pa and I asked." And asked and asked.

"Ah." Bell gave him a little salute and then headed off to get his horse ready.

The thing keeping him from continuing to bunk in town was the thought of encountering Miss Juliana Beauchamps daily. She didn't scare him, not exactly, but she put him on edge. He'd never been one to compare himself—had too much of that with others comparing his height to theirs'—but now he found himself criticizing his own appearance.

He headed to the side of his cabin and grabbed some firewood then ducked inside the door. He needed to keep focused on his job. But after setting his wood down, he stepped to the slab wood table and lifted the Milwaukee newspaper he'd picked up in town. He'd left it open to the society section.

James Yost, one of our most prominent citizens, has departed on what is described by his social secretary as both a "business and pleasure" trip into Michigan's eastern Upper Peninsula. His presence will be missed at our society functions here. Until he returns...

What business did a man like Yost have around here? And what kind of pleasure was he seeking?

Richard set the Milwaukee paper aside and settled into the rocker. He read part of a newer Sherlock Holmes book, *The Sign of Four*. Now every noise had him wondering what or who was out there. Even three kerosene lamps wouldn't deter the darkness that would overcome the cabin within an hour.

Over the sound of crackling wood, he could have sworn he'd heard women's voices. Ma always claimed he had the best imagination of the three of them. Couldn't be female voices he heard. The only ladies who'd come out to the camp were the handful who'd come out from town early on to see where they'd be working—and promptly returned to St. Ignace. That was one of the reasons he'd taken to interviewing in town.

Someone rapped at the door and Richard jumped up, threw off the quilt covering his lap, and reached for his shotgun.

"Mr. Christy! It's the Beauchamps." Was that giggling he heard?

He sucked in a deep breath and laid his weapon aside. After lifting the latch, he opened the door.

Juliana stood there holding a basket, with a taller young woman with golden hair, and an older lady, peering in.

The silver-haired woman smiled up at him. "I'm your neighbor, Nora Beauchamps."

He gestured for them to enter. "I believe you're the one to thank for sending Mr. Bell my way, ma'am. Please come on in."

"Thank you."

"Neighbors are ya?" They must live as close as Bell had suggested. He waved them in and as they passed, he smelled something beefy. "Smells like pasties to me, is it?"

"You've got a good sniffer, young man."

"My favorite, ma'am." His mouth watered as the scents of beef, potato, onion and turnips mingled in his new little home. Wasn't much to it and sure wasn't like the Yost mansion, pictured in the society article. Good thing he had four ladderback chairs by the table. "Have a seat?"

Miss Beauchamps beamed up at him. "I thought I'd heard your lumber camp was right near our home."

"Actually, it's a few miles." The blonde woman slowly lowered herself into a seat, as though she were stiff. "And I'm Claudette Beauchamps, Mr. Christy."

"Welcome to my cabin. Can I make you some coffee?" At least his tins were all clean since they were new from Labrons.

"No, thanks..." She untied her bonnet.

"I'd love some." Miss Juliana Beauchamps removed her fussy-looking black hat trimmed with gray bird feathers.

He went to his pantry and retrieved the fixings and catsup for the pasty and then poured water into the percolator and set it on the woodstove. "This could take a little while ladies. Are you joining me for dinner, then?"

"Oh no, we've already eaten, but Juliana thought you might enjoy some." Mrs. Beauchamps glanced between the two of them.

The blonde flexed her shoulders. "She worked very hard on them."

Was it his imagination or was Juliana frowning? She'd averted her gaze and now stood.

Mrs. Beauchamps smoothed her hair. "Juliana's such a hard worker, I don't know what I'd do without her."

"What would we both do, Mama?" Claudette dropped her chin to her chest and closed her eyes for a moment.

"Yes, well, you shan't have to know..." Juliana called over her shoulder as she removed her coat and hung it from a peg on the wall. When she turned, she'd pasted a bright smile on her face but her eyes were sad.

Mrs. Beauchamps reached across the table and patted his hand. "I imagine you know, Mr. Christy, that she works as a librarian all day long."

"Yes'm, I do." Those pasties smelled delicious and his mouth watered.

Mrs. Beauchamps must have read his mind because she pushed her parcel toward him. "You better eat before these get any colder."

"She packed three for you." Claudette now swiveled her head from side to side. She reminded him of someone. Grandma Christy, with rheumatism, that's who.

All eyes trained on him as he took his first bite. Then he had to slow himself so he didn't devour the meat pie. He almost groaned, the savory taste was so pleasant and so much better than beans and hard tack and dried buns he'd been eating.

"Juliana made that. She does all our cooking." Claudette, the pretty blonde, appeared in her mid to late twenties, and must be Juliana's older sister. Why didn't she help? Maybe she was infirm— certainly looked to be.

"We help—we peel, cut, chop during the afternoon, but it's our Juliana who does the actual cooking when she gets home." Mrs. Beauchamp set her hands on the table. Her gnarled fingers were swollen around the knuckles and red. She must be in a fair amount of pain with that rheumatism. He'd seen it before. Pa feared it could happen to him if he kept at the lumbering trade—it was one reason Pa wanted out before he became old before his time. This lady, though, appeared to be closer to seventy--maybe near Grandma's age. And something was wrong with her daughter, too. What a shame.

Juliana cleared her throat. "Of course the two of you do the majority of the work. I just throw it together and put it in the oven." She pushed another pasty toward him and he placed it on his plate.

"Delicious, Miss Beauchamps."

Her face reddened as deep as the catsup he'd opened and was spreading over the meat pastry. Did she think he'd said she was delicious? His own cheeks heated.

"This here meal tastes wonderful."

She nodded, her eyebrows raised and her mother glanced between the two of them. He lowered his head and focused on shoveling his food in. When all grew quiet, he slowed and raised his head. All three women laughed.

"Good to see a man with a hearty appetite." Mrs. Beauchamps continued to chuckle and wiped away a tear from her eyes.

"No menfolk at your place, ma'am?" His shoulders stiffened—if they lived that close and were unprotected, how did they manage? And although the sheriff confirmed Bell's military connection, he wondered if the rest was correct.

"We have a brother who fishes in Naubinway and he comes by sometimes." Juliana's tone was defensive, like she expected an argument.

"And one of my sons is moving his family back soon from the mines."

"What?" Juliana cocked her head at her mother.

"Yes, Phillip."

"He's bringing my grandson and his little family with him, too." The woman patted her daughter's hand, across the table. "Don't worry dear, they've both procured jobs at the mill."

"Yes," Claudette agreed. "They're finally coming back home."

Juliana's lower lip worked, as though she was chewing it. *Mighta been nice if her kinfolk had informed her about her brother.*

"Good to have work, ma'am." Richard took another bite.

Claudette shifted in her chair. "I'm hoping to find employment, too, one day."

Pretty girl like her should be married. Maybe her condition kept fellas away.

Mrs. Beauchamps pushed the third pasty at him. "Juliana takes care of me and Claudette. She's a good girl."

He stopped chewing when he heard the librarian's sharp intake of breath. "Mother, please."

"What? I'm giving you well due praise, Juliana." Wind rattled the cabin's shutters and seeped through the walls. Would need to chink those in better.

So was Mrs. Beauchamps warning him away from her daughter? "My pa thinks I'm a good son, too, ma'am, although I can't say why. He's trusting me to get this lumber camp in order and I've got my work cut out for me, as you can see." For one thing, no one wanted to cook.

Chuckling, Claudette stood and stretched. "You'd never get Juliana out here unless you add some pretty flowers. Maybe some lilacs."

"Beggin' to differ, Miss, but Juliana is here right now." He grinned and took another bite and the librarian narrowed her eyes at him.

Claudette moved toward the stove and extended her hands.

"There is nothing of beauty in this place, Mr. Christy." Juliana lifted her chin. "I see no flowers planted, not even daffodils, and no lilac bushes nor other flowering trees."

He had beauty there right now. He kept chewing, looking into her blazing blue eyes. What would it be like to look at that pretty face every night? "Flowers are gonna bring ladies out here?"

Maybe he needed to see the place as a woman would. He'd have to ask his sister, too.

Mrs. Beauchamps chuckled. "Good pay, a safe and respectful place, and yes, gussy it up some and that might help the town ladies see some potential here."

"Lilacs, there have to be lilacs for this to be a place I'd want to visit." Juliana squared her shoulders.

That stuck in his craw. Lilacs gave him sneezing fits. No way in tarnation was he ever putting in lilacs. "Right sorry to hear that Miss Beauchamps."

Right sorry indeed! The only one sorrier than her was Mother, who now kept her eyes glued to the red-and-white checked tablecloth. So, he was saying he didn't want her out here. She'd fix him. When the lilacs bloomed she'd have them on her desk daily. And she and Claudette would be bringing some lilac bushes out. "We should get going, Mr. Christy."

Between her mother's and Claudette's comments, Richard likely thought her an old maid saddled with the responsibility for her family. With kerosene light pooling circles in several corners of the rustic building, something whispered to her heart. Juliana was yet unmarried and the caretaker of her sister and mother. Such had been her fate when her fiancé, Aleksanteri Puumula, had left her to supposedly pursue a future for them near the mines in the western part of the peninsula. A second generation Finlander, Alek had been the best student in school. How he'd look down his perfect nose at Richard if he met him, even though Aleksanteri, too, had been brought up in a lumber camp.

"Mrs. Beauchamps, I found a hoard of canning jars in the cook house and since I don't even have cooks..." Their host clamped his mouth into a line then took a long drink of his coffee.

"Yet." Claudette bobbed her head and smiled. Her sister was so beautiful. With the lamplight gleaming on her hair, would Richard be drawn to her? But he took another swig of coffee and seemed to be lost in thought.

"That's right." Mother covered the lumberjack's hand with her own. "God hasn't sent you the right ladies yet. And yes—we'd love to have those canning jars. Why last year we sold enough jars to put aside for both the girls' weddings."

Money aside? Weddings? Juliana felt her mouth drop open.

Richard began to choke on his coffee, but in a moment stopped and patted at his lips with the red cotton cloth he used for a napkin. He gazed directly into Juliana's eyes, a muscle in his face twitching. "Why Miss Beauchamps, I didn't reckon you were engaged to someone." He ran a finger around his black and red checked collar.

Her mother laughed as Juliana cringed. "She's not yet—just like the cooks you don't have yet, Mr. Christy."

"I'm not betrothed, either." Claudette lowered her head. "And unlike Juliana, who has been engaged, I doubt I'll ever be."

Juliana shot her younger sister a searing glance hoping to silence her, but Claudette didn't look up so she averted her gaze only to find Richard staring at her.

"As yer Ma said, not yet, Miss."

What must Richard think of her mother and sister? "Well, we better go before it gets dark."

"I'll ride out with you, ladies."

"No need." Her mother waved a dismissive hand.

"Yes'm, there's every need. Ya got precious cargo there in yer girls." He stood and first offered their coats to them and then donned his own. "That way, too, I can run them jars over to ya sometime, as I'll know where ya live."

Soon they were hopping into the carriage, assisted by Richard. Claudette loved to drive and she got in first, followed by their mother. When it was Juliana's turn, Richard turned her to face him. She craned to look up at him. Even in the twilight, she could read his expression, and it took her breath away. He cast a look that a suitor wore when he was falling in love.

"Miss Beauchamps, I'm so glad ya came out here."

Heart hammering, she managed to nod.

"And thank ya kindly for the victuals. And for being a good neighbor to a lumberjack."

"You're welcome." The heat from his hands seeped through her gloved hands.

He didn't release her, but stepped in closer, his breath forming puffs in the chilly night air. "And don't believe I'm thinkin' any less of ya despite what yer ma and sister said."

"Thank you." The scent of woodsmoke mingled with leather and a strong, but not unpleasant, soap.

Wind whispered through the nearby pines.

"You're no old drone. And you're too lovely to be keepin' company with the likes of me—a shanty boy. Yet ya show me kindness at every turn, for which I'm right grateful." He still held her hands and showed no inclination to release them. Mother cleared her throat and Juliana pulled free.

Mr. Christy, you may be saying one thing, but your behavior says something else entirely. She grinned. "Just follow us home, then." She'd be the belle of the Lumberjacks' Ball, with the handsomest lumberjack escorting her. Then all those tongues that wagged over Alek leaving her behind would be stilled.

"First let me help ya up, Juliana." In one fell swoop, he'd lifted her and placed her gently inside the back of the buggy.

Her heart pounded in her chest despite the fact that she hadn't needed to exert herself whatsoever. He'd lifted her like she was a bit of fluff. What would it be like to have someone take care of her? Dare she allow herself to imagine?

Chapter 4

Late May

After securely locking the library's doors, Juliana met Gracie and the orphans in front of the building. Spring had finally arrived in the Straits of Mackinac and daffodils and crocuses were popping up in red and yellow masses against the fledgling green grass. Winds blew off the water briskly, setting a nearby flag to flapping wildly against its pole.

Virginia clutched her hat, an odd-shaped little covering that resembled an acorn and fit her impish personality. "Why are you walking us back to the orphanage, Miss Beauchamps?" There was a tease in the child's voice. Did she know about the gown Juliana had made for a dance that she'd not yet been invited to?

Juliana teased back, "I suppose it's because I'm going to adopt all of you and take you out into the country to live with a hundred dogs and a thousand cats."

When a tiny flicker of hope appeared and then disappeared from the child's eyes, a stab of regret pierced Juliana. *What careless words.* If she had her way, she'd take a half dozen orphans home with her. How wonderful it would be to be surrounded by children again. Soon her older brother would arrive with his family. But there was plenty of room where she lived. "Do you know something?"

The child shrugged and averted her eyes to the walkway.

"I wonder if Sister Mary Lou might let some of you come to visit with us—maybe some of you children could take turns coming out every week." But how would they feed all those extra mouths? She wished she could trust God, but seeing as

He took away her fiancé all those years ago and her brothers, she didn't count on Him to provide. Maybe if she'd not spent so much money on her gown then she wouldn't be worrying about feeding extra mouths. But something about her Bon Jean had her wanting to attend the Lumberjacks' Ball. And she would attend that dance and make sure that those who'd tormented her after Aleksanteri abandoned her would see that Juliana Beauchamps wasn't a washed up old spinster.

They marched along, the children talking and laughing amongst themselves. Stephen and Marcus Lone slipped their hands in Juliana's. "We want to be the first to go to your house."

"And together." The blond twin fixed his green gaze on her.

"We'll see. Father Paul has to approve." Sister Mary Lou would agree, Juliana knew that in her heart, but the priest had to answer to the diocese and to the orphanage board. Hopefully, there was no one on the committee like Mr. Hatchens.

When she stopped in front of Josephine Christy's bakery, the children broke ranks and ran to the windows, pressing their hands and noses to the glass.

"We're praying for Miss Christy and her father." Virginia clasped her small hands together.

Timmy pointed to the "Closed" sign. "Father Paul says it's a shame Miss Christy had to close her store, to go see if her dad is all right, but he said that's what family does for each other."

"Yeah." Marcus hugged his twin. "And Sister Mary Lou says I'm blessed because I have family right with me."

Stephen elbowed his twin and wriggled free then raised his fists. "Not if you're gonna hug me in public. Unless you want to be blessed with a shiner."

Gracie strode to Marcus and pulled him against her side. She pointed to the back of the line.

Juliana lifted her whistle, dangling from a chain on her chatelaine, and blew sharply. A dozen startled faces turned in her direction. "Any child who is back in line, and proceeds quietly and with decorum into the store, will receive a treat."

A collective gasp went up before quick feet brought them back in queue. Gracie laughed but wagged a finger at them. "All of you behave."

After she unlocked the door, Juliana turned to face the orphans as passersby gawked at them. "Miss Josephine Christy has offered us her unsold cookies." Hopefully they were all the same type because if they weren't, the children might argue over them. She stepped inside and approached the case and scanned it. A huge stack of sugar cookies overflowed a platter. *Perfect.*

Gracie cleared her throat. "Wipe your feet as you enter."

The boys made a show of repeatedly wiping their feet while the girls rolled their eyes at them and giggled.

The twins moved to the front of the line, waving their hands.

"Yes, Stephen?"

The dark-haired twin grinned until a dimple showed on his chubby cheek. "Can we pray for Miss Christy's family?"

Was Stephen trying to redeem himself for his early misbehavior? "Yes, let's bow our heads for a moment."

As silence fell over the group, remorse filled Juliana. Her actions of late had been about what she wanted. She'd not been thinking of the Christy family. She should have been praying for all of them the minute Josephine and Rebecca asked her and Richard to watch over their stores. Instead, she'd made cow eyes at Richard, who was beside himself worried over his brother and father. Although Richard denied his distress when they'd talked about watching over the shop, the way his jaw muscle jumped and his fists clenched had told her otherwise. And she'd spoken no words of faith to him.

"Juliana?" Gracie's whisper brought her back to the moment.

"Yes, I'm sorry. Dear Father in heaven, we thank you for these children. Give them all good homes." A tear slipped down her cheek. The words had just slipped out. "And be with the Christy family. All of them." *Richard, too, and let me be of support to him.* "Give them safety in their travels, and where there is illness in this situation, bring healing. In Jesus's name, Amen."

She wiped her face with the back of her hand and headed behind the counter as the children glued their eyes on the cookies.

"I wish I could come here every day." Marcus's mouth hung slack as he stood by the glass case.

As she passed a treat to each child, in turn, Juliana couldn't help but be touched further by their grateful smiles and joyous reactions. Did God ever look down on her and wonder why she didn't rejoice when he'd done something in her life? He'd given her the opportunity for schooling and a job when Aleksanteri departed without her. God had used Juliana to provide for her sister and mother when Papa had died. Now he'd brought this family of friends into her life— feisty Josephine who always spoke the truth in love, the talented Garrett whose hands crafted beautiful furniture from the very wood he used to cut down, and Richard who seemed to love books and children as much as she did.

The orphans hadn't bothered to sit in the chairs that surrounded small tables in the store. Instead, they'd almost inhaled their cookies.

Juliana shook her head. "Some of you have more cookie on you than made it in your little mouths."

"Or on the floor?" Steven laughed and wiped his face with his coat sleeve.

"I'll sweep up after them." Gracie gestured to a broom and dustpan that peeked from behind the open doorway to the back storage room.

When the last child had finished and the floor was swept, they left and Juliana relocked the door. Tomorrow she'd take some vinegar water to the front windows to remove the hand and nose prints. Which of these precious imps would she bring home first? And wouldn't they cheer up Mother!

Their delight in the simple act of receiving a cookie had encouraged her soul. Maybe Claudette, too, would find the same thing by watching their actions. Maybe something outside herself was just what her sister needed.

Soon they'd reached the orphanage. Sister Mary Lou's dark habit flapped around her as she descended the steps to greet them. "Has the Secret Cookie Festival been successful?"

The children cheered and the nun beamed. She took Juliana's arm and pulled her aside as Gracie and the children ascended the stairs. "It's done."

"My dress?" She'd squealed so loudly that several children swiveled around. Juliana covered her mouth, then quickly dropped her hand.

"Just a few finishing touches. But I've got a key and I'll put it in the armoire to surprise Miss Hart when she returns."

"I can hardly wait to see it!" She trembled with excitement. Would Mrs. Puumala be at the Lumberjacks' Ball? Would she and her husband wonder why their son hadn't married her?

For ten long years she'd endured the pitying looks of her friends as they added child after beautiful child to their homes and spoke of how accomplished their husbands were at work. And had she heard anything from Aleksanteri?

You need to let this go. The words were almost audible and Juliana scanned the nearby church building, its stained glass windows glowing softly in the afternoon sun. She shivered. God was preparing her heart. She and Alek had been so young.

Sudden tears pricked her eyes but she wiped them away. "I have to go." *I have to let Aleksanteri's hurt go, too.*

Juliana hadn't slept well as she'd wrestled with hanging onto her anger and resentment but by morning, she'd given Alek over to God along with her hurt feelings. But now, settled in the workroom at the library, she clutched her copy of

Sonnets of the Portuguese to her breast and sipped a third cup of Earl Grey tea. Glancing downward at the note from Mr. Yost, she took in his quickly scrawled words about meeting with him to discuss filing systems. She set the Elizabeth Barrett Browning book onto the rectangular worktable and took her tea cup and cookie with her to the glass windows that overlooked the street. This was the St. Ignace she knew from her youth. But soon it would be teeming with wealthy tourists and seasonal occupants. Despite the heavy fog this morning, she knew that even now porters lugged early arrivals' trunks up from the docks. She dipped one of Josephine's sugar cookies into the steaming brew then took a bite. Not stale at all now. Amazing how something dry and brittle could take on new life so easily.

The distinctive form of Richard Christy emerged through the mist, setting her pulse racing. Could he infuse her heart with a new beginning? She glanced down at her keys, hanging from the chatelaine on her chest. Richard possessed the key to Rebecca's shop. Might Juliana's gown be in the armoire as Sister Mary Lou said? What did it look like? Was it as perfect as she imagined? Oh, what she'd give to try it on—or at least look at it completely done. And she'd dance at the ball with Richard. No longer would her motivation include anything to do with Aleksanteri and her need to prove to the community that she wasn't a cast-off spinster.

Grabbing her sweater, she raced out of the building to meet him on the walkway. "Good morning, Mr. Christy." She pressed a hand to her chest, hoping to still her rapid heartbeat.

He set down his canvas bag, overflowing with books, and ran a hand back through his dark hair. "Mornin'. How ya doin' today?"

"I'm fine, just fine." Except she was bobbing up and down on her toes like a schoolgirl. She forced herself to still. "I'm about to take a short break, and I was wondering if I might have the key to Miss Hart's mercantile?"

A frown tugged between his eyebrows. "I was gonna go down there myself in a few minutes, but I reckon that would be all right."

"Good for me to stretch my legs with this lovely weather we're having. Once that fog burns off later we should have another sunny day."

He fished a key from his vest pocket and handed it to her, the metal warm from his body. Richard pressed it into her hand then sandwiched her much smaller palms between his, the strength and heat in them speeding up her heartbeat even further. As he leaned in, she held her breath. Was he going to kiss her? Not out here in public. Strands of wavy hair fell across his broad forehead. Something shifted in her—his brow was completely unlined. His cheeks smooth above his beard. No lines etched yet around his eyes. How was that possible?

"Miss Beauchamps, please don't go in the mercantile's back area—Ox will have my hide if you do. Better yet—wait a few minutes for my long legs to catch up with you after I return these here books." He bent and picked up the rucksack.

She clutched the key. "See you there."

Across the street, the busy harbor held the first of the regular ferryboats that crossed to Mackinac Island. As soon as Richard lumbered toward the library building, Juliana raced down the walkway, wishing she flew faster than any cannonball that had ever shot from Fort Mackinac, over the straits. When would the rest of the Christy family return over those cerulean waters?

When she arrived at the mercantile, she hesitated only a moment, eying the sign advertising for lumber camp cooks. Poor Richard still hadn't found any. She'd start asking her friends if they knew of anyone.

She unlocked the door and admitted herself into the mercantile, which reeked of fumes even worse this day. Was it lamp oil? Or was Ox careless with his varnish and turpentine? She waved her hand before her face. Maybe she should reopen the door, but she'd only be here a minute or two.

Juliana's heart throbbed in anticipation. Her heart pumped in her chest. Because of the strong odor, she had difficulty drawing a breath. With the light streaming through the front windows, she didn't need to adjust the gaslights.

From the back of the shop something skittered and she cringed. She hated mice. Waiting, she heard nothing further and moved forward.

Every muscle in her body tensed in anticipation as she headed to the beautiful armoire that Garrett had constructed. She threw it open. *Empty. Completely barren. Nary a gown to be seen.* Her heart sank. Disappointment coursed through her, freezing her there. She closed the door reluctantly, a floorboard creaking nearby.

"Here for the store owner," a sinister voice sounded from the back. "You there, Janie?"

She whirled around as a whoosh sounded, bringing with it smoke.

"Here to finish what I started." An emaciated-looking man flew toward her, tugging on a hank of rope.

Juliana shook her head and backed up.

"You're not the mercantile owner. Not my Janie." His wild eyes flashed like a wounded beast's.

"No. I'm not Janie." Who was Janie? She had to get out.

The shaggy-haired creature began to scream, as though the hounds of hell had found him.

She moved past him toward the door but when she reached for the handle, she, too, screamed, in pain, as the brass doorknob burned her hand. She stumbled backward several steps, tripped over her hem, and fell to the floor, crying out in pain as the man's clawlike hand gripped her throat.

What Richard should have been doing was meeting with more ladies for the cook job but instead, he'd spent the early morning swilling coffee and chowing on baked goods at Cordelia's inn. Now he hurried to catch up with Juliana. Today was the day he'd tell her that she wouldn't be seeing much of him anymore. He was young. He had plenty of time to get married. What in tarnation was he thinking now? They'd not even begun courting and already he was begging off marrying her? She'd think he was a lunatic. Better just to stay far away from her.

From three blocks back, the fog broke and the sun beat down. He could see Juliana, straight ahead of him, entering the mercantile. Hadn't she paid him any never mind when he told her to wait on him? Women—so stubborn—another reason he couldn't get married right now. He rubbed the side of his head, which began to ache. Both he and Ox had been on edge because of Peevey's release and now the question of who was encamped in the old cabin near the camp. But, it was daytime, and who could figure out a woman's rationale for why she did the things she did?

Richard opened the door and smoke rolled toward him. He narrowed his eyes against the fumes' assault and saw someone grabbing Juliana. He rushed in. Myron Peevey shrieked like a maniac. Richard knocked him down. "Get out, Juliana."

But she lay there as fire crackled up from Ox's workroom.

A searing blow caught him in the eye and he stifled a groan. Richard punched Peevey back as the flames licked forward.

Grabbing Juliana, he whirled and charged out into the street as the building burst into flames behind them. Something within the building crashed and he ran faster.

"Get back! Get the Fire Brigade!" he yelled at two men on the walkway, and they turned and ran toward the docks. As a blast shook the block, he fell down atop the librarian, trying to brace himself with his arms and legs so as not to hurt her.

"Oh God," he leant up on his forearms, his knees on either side of her as debris rained down on them. He bent closer and seeing her uninjured, he kissed Juliana's damp forehead.

"Richard," she whispered, eyes wide.

"Oh God, oh my Lord," he repeated as he pressed his lips to her forehead again, which was wet with something. Where were the tears coming from? Seeing that murderous Peevey with Juliana had snapped something loose in him and cloaked him with the presence of the Holy Spirit.

Juliana reached up and wiped moisture from his face. "You saved me."

"No, Miss Beauchamps, God did." Why? Twice in his life now, he'd helped rescue a young woman from that insane man, who surely now was dead.

"I'm glad..." She took a shaky breath beneath him. "He let you be part of it."

Whistles and bells pierced the air. From up the street, a fire carriage lurched forward as volunteers streamed from nearby businesses, merchants jumping up onto the side as it passed.

He began to cough as the air filled with dust. "We need to move further back." They could have been killed. He had to get Juliana away to avoid more injury.

Picking Juliana up, he carried her down the walkway as black matter rained down on them. She leaned her head into his neck and a fierce protectiveness shot through him. No one was going to hurt Miss Juliana Beauchamps again, if he had any say over it.

What would he have done if she'd died? His arms began to shake, not from her feather-light weight, but from the crevice that had formed in his heart and which a tiny librarian had crawled inside. Life was short. He of all people should know that, even at his age.

He inclined his head toward the ladies gawking at them as he brought Juliana to a bench. Richard set her down and then sat beside her, wrapping an arm around her shaking shoulders. She leaned in against him. Truth be told—it felt like the most natural thing in the world, despite the circumstances.

A gust of wind carried the stench of the fire away from them. In a moment of clarity, his spirit knew God called

Richard back to Him, as if the words, "Come close, son," had been spoken.

Juliana raised her head and looked up at him, as if she'd heard the soul whisper, too.

He pressed her head back to his shoulder. "I guess we're gonna have to go to that Lumberjacks' Ball together now."

Chapter 5

A knock on the door roused Juliana from her fitful nap. She pulled the white counterpane coverlet up around her neck. Gazing around the room, she remembered that she was in a bedchamber at Cordelia Jeffries' inn.

Across the room, seated in the poufed boudoir chair in the corner, her sister's eyes fluttered open. Claudette blinked several times, as though she, too, was trying to orient herself. "Who is it?"

"Physician."

"Come in!"

With efficient movements, a tall, chestnut-haired stranger entered, a dark browned leather satchel clutched in one large hand.

"I'm Dr. Ellison Adams-Payne." The man's clipped British accent surprised Juliana.

"Oh?" Her burned hands still ached terribly, despite the laudanum.

The physician pushed his spectacles up his straight nose and smiled, a small cleft marking a firm chin set in a square jaw.

Claudette attempted to rise, her stiff movements unproductive. "Thank you for coming, doctor."

Straight dark eyebrows rose over deep brown eyes as Dr. Adams-Payne gazed at Juliana's sister. "Did you spend the night in that chair, madam?" He took Claudette's hand in his and assisted her up.

"No, I did not." She patted at her skirts, which were a wrinkled mess.

He frowned and raised her hand toward the gaslight on the wall and tilted his head first one way and then another.

"And it is Miss, not Madam, doctor." Blushing, Claudette tugged her hand free. "You're here to examine my sister's hands, not mine."

A smile tugged at the handsome man's lips and he moved toward the bed. "Mr. Christy asked me to look in on you, Miss Beauchamps."

"How is he this morning?"

"Fine." His generous mouth became a firm line. "I am 'told' by him that he is perfectly fine to return to his camp, regardless of my professional opinion."

Juliana laughed. "That sounds like him." She settled her head further back on the down-stuffed pillow and relaxed.

What a strange sensation it had been to be waited on in bed at Cordelia's inn the past day. And knowing Richard was only a few doors down the hall. A blessing and torment at the same time.

Dr. Adams-Payne removed her gauze wrappings and examined her hands. "I studied in London, under some rather famous physicians."

His features were placid and there was no braggadocio in his measured words.

"Yes? And?"

"Beside learning which compounds healed burns..." He opened his satchel, removed a jar and opened it. "...I researched conditions causing inflammation in the body—such as in the finger joints."

Claudette narrowed her eyes at the doctor, but he wasn't looking at her. What was bothering her sister?

When the physician gently applied the salve, Juliana pressed her eyes shut, the stinging sensation painful.

"Take a deep breath, my dear Miss Beauchamps, while I reapply your bandages." Thankfully, his British accent distracted her. "And the other Miss Beauchamps, might you move out of the gaslight, please, and come closer? I wish to address you."

Juliana heard Claudette's gasp.

"Address me? I've not asked to speak with you. And while I appreciate your help for my sister, you have no medical business with me." Where had her compliant and complacent Claudette fled? The woman in the room with her possessed a tart, rather than sweet, tongue.

"Don't I, though?" The physician secured Juliana's bandage and swiveled to face Claudette. "I've been paid to give a consultation as to your condition."

"What?" Claudette's pretty mouth formed an outraged "O" as she glared at the handsome young doctor.

"Indeed, my dear young woman."

"I am not…"

The doctor held up a hand to stop her. "And from the history I've been given, and from what I see today, I'd like to make some recommendations."

Claudette crossed her arms. Behind her the door opened and Richard entered, dressed in a black and red checked flannel shirt and work pants, his suspenders hanging down from his shoulders. He hastily tugged them up.

"I heard ya fussin', Claudette—what's got yer dander raised?"

He called her sister by her given name? And yet he'd continued to refer to Juliana as Miss Beauchamps? She glanced between the two, her discomfort building in her spirit rather than in her burned hands.

"This…this…stranger," her younger sister pointed to Dr. Adams-Payne, "thinks he can waltz in here and instead of focusing his attentions on Juliana, he wants to diagnose and treat me." She tapped one booted foot.

"Well, I reckon that's 'cause I asked him to. Me and yer Ma agreed." Richard took Claudette's elbow and led her back to the chair. "Now listen up to what this here fella tells ya, because he's been trained under special doctors over in England. Docs who know all about what makes people get all stiff and sore like you and yer ma get."

Clearing his throat, the Englishman moved toward Claudette while Richard slipped back out the door. "May I suggest a few things, miss?"

"I suppose."

"Have you tried willow bark tea?"

"Yes, but we don't have it regularly."

"Have some daily."

"We'll see."

Dr. Adams-Payne scowled at her pretty sister. "How about cod liver oil?"

Claudette made a face. "No, I detest it."

He took her hand and pressed. She winced. "If you want this to improve, I'd recommend you try at least a tablespoon morning and night. Might that be agreeable?"

She nodded.

"And get out in the fresh air—sunshine may help, though we aren't sure how."

"That's what you consider medical advice? I'm outside with the orphans who visit my home each weekend."

He chuckled. "Yes, that's my advice, and get outside daily, and walking would be good for you, too, to strengthen you and improve your constitution."

Her constitution? She'd never seen her sister act so perturbed before—except maybe when Aleksanteri had run off and left Juliana.

"All right. I'll try all that for one month." Claudette's voice, however, made no promises. "And one month only."

Richard ducked his dark head back in the door. "Hey, Doc, I'm not one to be remindin' people, but did ya bring that pain medication—that special powder—so Miss Beauchamps can rest easier without being so…" He made a whirling motion with his hand. "We've had some bad experiences at the camp with laudanum."

"I apologize for my delay. I fear I have a strong scholarly interest in inflammatory conditions, which has distracted me." Red crept up the physician's cheeks.

Whether the doctor genuinely was fascinated by Claudette's illness or whether he'd been more interested in her beautiful face and figure, Juliana couldn't say. But she did know she needed something for the pain. "Claudette, could you get me some water, please?"

Dr. Adams-Payne fumbled with the latch on his case. "Let me retrieve the powder I compounded for Miss Beauchamps."

"Reckon that's why I called ya in here, doc." Richard glanced between her sister and the doctor, a crease forming between his eyebrows.

Was he jealous of the interest the physician showed her sister?

Richard slipped into the back row of the county building's main auditorium for the Library Trustees' meeting. He'd not been quite honest with the doc—he'd had no intention of riding out to the camp—he'd planned to attend this "special" meeting that old Hatchens had cooked up for that night. Mrs. Jeffries had informed him earlier, "That carbuncle on humanity is up to something and has called a meeting of the board."

The large space was almost empty, save for the dozen or so men who sat at a rectangular table at the dais on the stage. Hatchens stood in the center, shuffling through a folder. He pulled his pocket watch out and then reached for a gavel. He brought it down with a "bang" causing the man in front of Richard to jerk awake in his chair. James Yost. What was he doing there? And why was the man pushing himself so hard when obviously he should be in his room sleeping? On the other hand, why wasn't he, himself, resting back at the inn? Were they both there for the petite librarian? Richard clenched his fists as he eyed the finely dressed beer baron. Why was the wealthy man always tailing after Juliana at the library, asking questions about someone named Dewey?

Up front, Hatchens pointed to one of the other members. "You have Miss Beauchamps contract with you, don't you, Cyrus?"

The man nodded.

"Fine. Let me commence."

Charles Labron, the store proprietor, took a seat nearby and lifted his hand in greeting.

"First, I'm sure all are aware that our librarian, Miss Juliana Beauchamps, was injured in the terrible fire that nearly destroyed our main thoroughfare yesterday."

Labron mumbled, "Our?" in disgust. With Hatchens a relative newcomer, apparently the store proprietor wasn't happy with his comment.

"And Miss Beauchamps has been injured with burns to her hands."

The member named Cyrus nodded. "She'll be unable to work for a short while."

Hatchens pushed aside his charcoal jacket and placed a fisted hand on his narrow hip. "And per her contract, we are not required to reimburse her, is that not correct, for any days absent due to sickness or injury or what have you." He rolled his eyes. What was Hatchens imagining that Juliana might be doing while she was out of work?

Cyrus scanned the papers before him. "That is correct."

Charles Labron abruptly stood and waved a hand. "I object. She has a lot on her shoulders. We should pay her while she's out."

"You're just wanting to ensure your bill gets paid, Mr. Labron." Hatchens snorted. "We'll hold a vote in a bit and see if your sentiment prevails or if reason does."

Labron slumped into his chair as Yost swiveled around. He briefly eyed Richard before lifting his chin at the store owner.

On the dais, two trustees at the far end of the table leaned in and began to converse. When Hatchens glared at them, they ceased.

"Further business—we need to seek out a temporary replacement."

All the men around the table nodded.

"We are expecting our interns, soon." Cyrus tapped a blue file folder. "All young men with impeccable credentials."

Sitting down, Hatchens' voice lowered and Richard strained to hear him. "Why the board chose to hire a woman as librarian is well beyond my ken."

Ahead of him, Yost's mouth tipped upward.

What in the world? Why was the beer baron happy about Hatchens' favoritism of male librarians?

"But the board made their decision before my arrival."

Labron stifled a snicker. "In the good old days."

As if he'd heard Labron's low remark, Hatchens stared in his direction. "And in Miss Beauchamps' case, I shall endeavor to ensure she does her job and does it well when she returns. That is, if she comes back at all."

And why wouldn't she?

How wonderful to be back in her own home, despite the many comforts of the inn. Juliana, Claudette, and Mother sat on a long bench out front of their home as the visiting orphans, Timmy, Stephen, and Marcus recited Edgar Allan Poe's spine-chilling poem, *The Raven*. She shivered. A man had died because of his pursuit of evil. Mr. Peevey could have embraced his freedom, but he'd sought to finish his murderous quest with Rebecca. A lone tear coursed down her cheek and she wiped it away. She paid rapt attention as they concluded their recitation. Then the women all clapped and the orphan trio bowed. How precious that the orphans came out to visit at her home during her recovery. They had read, sung, and gave little performances to distract her from her pain. But she had to get back to work—she needed to get paid.

Horses neighed as a dray pulled up the long sandy drive to the house. A wagon, stacked high with goods, came to a stop. Pierre, who shared the same name as her father and third eldest brother, was her old classmate and drove for their mutual friends, Janet and Charles Labron.

"Welcome, Pierre." Mother grinned up at him.

"Got a delivery for you, Mrs. Beauchamps."

She frowned. "But I didn't order anything."

Claudette rounded the dray, examining the contents, which appeared to be groceries.

Timmy climbed up the back, followed by Marcus and Stephen. "Look at all this food!"

"Boys!" Juliana followed after them, sighing. "This is a mistake."

Pierre laughed. "No mistake, Juliana."

How would she pay for it? Was Janet giving her a loan? Even so, how could she repay it?

Mother's eyes widened. "This is all for us?"

"Yes, it is." He hoisted a huge box from the back. "Where should I put everything?"

Claudette pointed to a spot on the stoop. "Did Mr. Christy send it?"

Juliana cringed. Why would her sister expect Richard to send anything? Yes, he'd kindly helped with the work around the place, and had brought fish he'd caught, which Claudette had fried up, but was there something blossoming between the lumberjack and her sister?

"No, miss, it's from Mr. Yost."

Yost? Oh no.

"He heard of that fusspot Hatchens' finagling to disallow Miss Juliana any pay while she was out." The drivers' jaw muscles twitched. "Don't see why some newcomer should be telling our Library Board what to do and not to do. And calling a special meeting the very next night after you were injured—well that's the lowest snake-belly thing yet, eh?"

Heat singed Juliana's cheeks.

"We agree." Her mother accepted a box of tinned goods and brought them to the cupboard.

"Sorry I couldn't get out before now, but it's a big order and we wanted to deliver it all together." Pierre uncrated a massive ham. "Yost ordered right after that meeting—before he left town."

Mother whirled around, a carton filled with precious tea, coffee, and sugar clutched in her hands. "Oh no, we won't be able to thank the kind man, then."

No more little messages would be left on her counter from Mr. Yost, asking if she might discuss filing systems with him. And of course, she'd had to oblige because part of her job as head librarian was assisting with research. But really, did a man have to make cow eyes at her when discussing the merits of various philosophies of library systems? Juliana wasn't sure if she should be relieved or sad that he had departed, but decided on the former.

By the next morning, when rich aromas of coffee and cinnamon baguettes permeated the morning air, Juliana was sorry she couldn't thank James Yost for his generosity. With mother's snores penetrating the wall between their bedchambers, it had to be Claudette who had risen to prepare the food. When she saw the physician, she would praise Dr. Adams-Payne, for his methods might be working. Mother wasn't usually up to such early rising, nor had poor Claudette been, until she'd begun Adams-Payne's regimen.

Juliana threw off the two pastel quilts that covered her single bed, tossed her braid over her shoulder, and pulled on her wrap. Then she padded out to the kitchen in her bare feet.

"Good morning, sister." Grinning, Claudette lifted the coffee pot from the stove and poured it into the steaming saucepan of milk adjacent. "You'll need to add sugar but I've thrown in a little cinnamon, too. And it's the premium Ceylon cinnamon—not the cheap stuff."

"*Merci.*" Juliana bobbed a little curtsey as a giggle bubbled up. Beside the fire, a nice stack of wood had been brought in. She pointed to it. "Your doing?"

"Yes." Claudette waved a wooden spoon like a wand. "Unless you think some wood sprite ran it up to the house for me."

After giving her younger sister a squeeze of appreciation, Juliana took her mug of café au lait, added two spoonsful of sugar, and brought it to the long table that used to sit their entire family of twelve. In the center lay a masterpiece of pastry, brown sugar and cinnamon. "This doesn't look like the usual breakfasts that I leave for you and Mother."

"Today, I feel so good I wanted to make something special for you and Mother." Claudette giggled. "And that rich Mr. Yost has made our feast possible."

Perhaps following the doctor's order was making the early rising and cooking possible, but Juliana dare not bring up Dr. Adams-Payne's name.

"I'm glad you feel better." Juliana laughed. "I'm going to enjoy the fruits of your energy."

"Please do—that's the point." Claudette pointed to a chair and Juliana sat down.

Her sister slid a spatula beneath a nice thick piece of the pastry and transferred it to Juliana's ironstone plate.

"Looks delicious." She pierced a chunk with her fork and brought it to her lips. Flaky perfection, cinnamon and caramelized sugar mingled and brought a sigh of appreciation from her. "Jo Christy has nothing on you, Claudette."

"That's what I am hoping, Sister." Claudette joined her at the table and cocked a blonde eyebrow.

"Oh?" Juliana lifted her coffee to her mouth, not wanting her sibling to see her concern.

"I've been feeling well enough to be active at least several hours in the morning as well as in the afternoon."

Juliana held the delicious beverage in her mouth not wanting to choke on it at her sister's words. While she was grateful for the progress, one had to be active far longer than only a few hours to be employable. She swallowed the hot liquid and watched as, instead of picking at her food, Claudette shoveled a large portion into her mouth. Who was this girl? And where was her sickly sister? Was she like Elizabeth Barrett Browning, whose sickliness was remedied by love? Or was it the physician's prescription?

"Richard cut the wood for us last night when Mother drove you and the children into town." A smiled tugged at her beautiful sister's lips.

Richard was it—not Mr. Christy? Juliana set her mug down, the contents sloshing like her stomach began to do. "Oh?"

"Yes. And he bought the last of our jams." Claudette pointed to a cloth bag of silver dollars.

"He did?" What else had he done that she didn't know about? Why wouldn't he come help her beautiful young sister?

They sat in silence, the wood fire crackling gently, the heat needed even on this late spring day. Juliana forced herself to keep eating, even though the pastry seemed to have turned to paper in her mouth.

She couldn't begrudge her sister anything. Not even Richard Christy if she'd set her cap for him. Juliana's pursuit of him was motivated by hurt and vanity. Wasn't it? Claudette and mother were the only family she had left in the area, for it seemed she'd lost her brother to drink years earlier. Mother was nearing seventy. Everywhere in the home there were signs of their mother's presence—from the crocheted antimacassars on the chairs, to the quilted multicolor placemats beneath their plates, to the chinaware from France. Yet Father's craftsmanship was here, too. He'd constructed the two-story home, which some said reminded them of a large hunting lodge. He'd built the dining table they sat at, and the chairs, as well as all the beds. And objects made by all the Beauchamps children decorated the large living space—paintings of lilacs she'd made in school, Claudette's clay bowl, Gerard's tiny cabin constructed of twigs, her brother Pierre's charcoal drawing of their grandfather fishing, and Pascal's horseshoe wreath that Mother still put out at Christmastime.

Yet no one here to care for Mother and Claudette. No one but Juliana. The Civil War had claimed three of her four older brothers. And it might as well have claimed Emmett, whom they rarely saw and when they did he was intoxicated. Juliana huffed out a sigh as she headed to bedroom to dress. Her eyes lighted on a picture propped on her bureau. Her brother, Pascal, beamed in the photograph taken with his crew. But he had died in a mining accident, leaving his widow, Melanie, and their three children. Hard to believe he'd be turning thirty-seven soon if he were alive.

Juliana donned her everyday clothing, pulling a loose, cotton, shift dress over her head. With care, she avoided any tugging that might aggravate her burned hands. What a blessing that she didn't require a frequent change in wardrobe and her librarian attire formed a simple uniform. Her brothers in military service would be attired in their regimentals. Sean and Connor had both enlisted in the U.S. Cavalry, despite Mother's and Father's protests, and moved out west with their units. If they sent their mother any money, she knew nothing of it. Their rare letters were scrutinized, as though they were holy writ, which Mother always studied as she did God's word, looking for hidden meaning. Would she ever see them again?

She wiped at a tear that coursed down her face. How did this house, once loud with the sound of men's voices, come to be a house occupied by only three women?

Juliana exited her bedroom.

A knock at the door startled her and she eyed the shotgun secured to the wall. As she moved toward the door, she called out, "Who's there?"

"Richard Christy here, Miss Beauchamps."

She opened the door to find him standing there, a string of fish hanging from his shoulder, feet bare and covered with sand, his pants legs rolled up revealing very hairy legs and muscular calves. Heat traveled up her neck and she pressed a hand there, as though doing so could staunch the red that would soon color her cheeks. Broad shoulders stretched an undershirt that emphasized his muscular chest, and she caught her breath.

He held out the line. "Brought you some more fish."

Struggling to speak, Juliana managed to say, "Thank you."

After lowering the fish into a bucket, he set it down and turned to her. "You all right?"

When she just blinked up at him, he gently took her hands in his and turned them over. He frowned. "Ain't ya been usin' that ointment?"

"Yes."

"And ya been restin'?"

"Resting my hands—if that's what you mean." She looked up into his dark eyes, so full of compassion.

Claudette tapped her from behind. Richard released her hands and Juliana moved aside to allow the prettier sister to come alongside her. "Why Richard, we're going to grow gills soon?"

Her sister's playful tone should have encouraged Juliana. She should be glad she was feeling better—but was she flirting? And with the man Juliana hoped would be her beau.

The big man laughed and he gently touched Juliana's neck, lifting her heavy curls, and sending a thrill through her. "I don't reckon I see any growin'—yet."

Heart hammering, Juliana was reminded of the terror she'd felt when that horrid man had choked her. She backed away and Richard's eyes widened.

Claudette took her arm, steadying her. "Are you dizzy?"

"No."

Richard shoved his hands in his pockets and averted his gaze, as though sensing her discomfiture. "How you feeling, Claudette? Ya think ya might be up to a little cookin' for my camp? I got a half dozen men arrived at camp and they're all clammerin' for good food."

Her sister's face lit up. She gestured toward the table. "Come sit and have some breakfast and we'll talk about it."

Juliana's jaw dropped open. How could Claudette possibly cook daily for a crew of men, even if currently that was limited? But her younger sister was an adult, so Juliana bit her tongue. Then she crossed her arms as Richard followed Claudette to the table.

"I've already eaten. I'm going for a walk." Juliana could feel the lumberjack's eyes on her back as she headed out the door. But what should have been a lovely walk to Lake Michigan, with gulls swooping and waves lapping at the shore, became a frightening experience as every caw startled her. Poor Rebecca. Was this what she'd had to endure?

Chapter 6

The Sunday school classroom seemed far smaller than Richard expected it to be—especially when surrounded by a dozen active boys. Was he so wild at their age? Yup. What had he agreed to?

The pastor's wife rang a small bell and then set it back on a tiny shelf built into the wall by Ox, for that very purpose. His older brother had some good ideas and that was one of them. If only he'd come back and work at the camp—it was not the same without him and Jo. But the rest of the crew would be there within a few months.

"Boys! Listen up! Mr. Christy is speaking today…"

A gap-toothed boy in a too-small shirt waved his arm. "Are we getting a Paul Bon Jean story today?"

Drats. He'd feared they'd expect a tall tale. But he'd come prepared. He lifted his Bible. "No sir, fellas, I got somethin' even better."

"Aw!" They sent up a collective sigh but he didn't flinch.

"I'm gonna talk about Goliath. But first I want to hear all of your names."

Mrs. Jones slipped out of the room.

The boys stood, one at a time, and recited their names. Richard tugged at his collar. How was he gonna remember 'em all? The last one stood, a gangly youth, his expression stoic. "Atlas Hatchens."

A couple of the boys whispered to one another and Richard cleared his throat. "Atlas, how 'bout you read from Samuel for us?"

The child complied, his pure, clear voice making the hair on Richard's arms stand on end. How could this youngster be the offspring of the vile man who tormented Juliana?

"Good job."

The boy's pale cheeks flushed.

"Can you explain the passage?"

"I believe so, sir. It's about how the Israelites had failed to obey God and hadn't killed all the giants in the land."

Matthew Labron raised his hand. "But if you'd lived back then, Mr. Christy, wouldn't they have killed you—you're a giant, aren't you?"

The boys laughed. Richard gestured for Atlas to take a seat.

"No sir, young Matthew, I wouldn't have been the Israelites' enemy. And there's a real good reason for that."

"Was it because they were over nine feet tall?" Matthew elbowed the boy beside him. "And you aren't?"

"Nope, it is because I believe in God and worship Him only."

The room quieted.

"It is true, I'm also no giant. I'm just a very tall man who was once your size." He pointed to each of them and winked. Granted, he'd been their size when he was years younger. He'd taken no small amount of teasing wherever they lived, even in the lumber camps.

"So we might grow as big as you?" A tall youth named Clark flexed his muscles.

Garrett laughed. "I've had to heft many an ax and fell many a tree to get these muscles." He flexed his biceps for them and their eyes got wide. "And if you're as big as me you have lots of daily difficulties."

"Like what?" Matthew cocked his head.

"Like fittin' in a bed, for one thing. My big brother is makin' me a new one for the lumber camp at Grand Corners." He'd tired of sleeping all cramped up with his feet hanging off the bed.

"You have a brother bigger than you?" Clark's mouth gaped open.

Richard ran his hand along his jaw. "My older brother, that is—not exactly bigger—just a figure of speech, I reckon."

"Oh." The boy slumped in disappointment.

"But as I was sayin', it ain't so good being too tall. If I get in a carriage, I have to duck my chin to my chest like this." He demonstrated. "When I come in a room I always have to check to be sure I'm not gonna get knocked out." He pointed to the doorway. "And I don't fit on most chairs." Like this one in which his knees were practically to his chest.

"Your brother's gonna make you chairs, too?" a child asked.

Had his great height influenced Ox to veer away from the lumberjack life, to which he'd seemed so suited, and to pursue furniture making? Why had God allowed that? "I 'spect so. But we need to get back to our Bible lesson. Who wants to be David?"

Matthew raised his hand and Richard had him read further in the passage. The boys sat still, which pleased him.

"So do you think this young brother, who was probably about you fellers' size, could bring down a big old giant?" Richard tapped the side of his head. "And from what Goliath was spoutin' off, what do ya think that bad old Philistine believed about himself?"

Clark popped up. "He thought he'd stomp him out." He stomped the floor.

"Get up fellas, we're gonna stomp like Goliath." Maybe that would chase some of their wiggles away.

Atlas Hatchens remained seated. "My father says men of strength are to be admired."

"Get up, Atlas." Matthew pulled him to his feet. "Your dad doesn't mean wicked men."

"Oh. Right." The slender boy smiled. "He says men of strong character should be admired."

"Well, now, we're gonna address that notion, too, young Atlas. What if a man had a strong character—say was a wealthy man of commerce..." like Yost "or a man who had great influence that he used to squash the hopes of others?" Like the boy's own father. "What then?"

The boy's pale face twisted. "I don't know."

Richard scrunched his face up in disbelief. The child clearly understood the Bible passage. "What if that high falutin' man went against God, Atlas?"

"He'd get a whoopin'," one of the boys called out.

Laughing, Richard held his hand high overhead, almost touching the ceiling. "Okay, fellas, let's say not only was Goliath physically massive but he's a man of influence, which some people misconstrue as character, which it ain't. And let's pretend that now he's stomping toward David." He pointed to Matthew to sit and led the class around him.

Matthew remained rooted as the boys encircled him, making ugly faces and growling at him.

"Okay, sit back down, fellas."

Behind him the door opened. He hoped they'd not distracted the other classrooms. "Read to us some more, Atlas." He handed the boy the Bible and pointed to the passage.

The trustee's son read how David, in his simple, yet strong faith in God, defeated the giant.

"First I want to make you all understand something before you leave. A man of character is someone who follows God's Word." He displayed the Bible. "He may not have two bits to rub together." He reached into his pocket and pulled out two coins and tossed one to Matthew and the other to Atlas. "Maybe he's a shanty boy who'll never be able to enjoy having young'uns like you all because he can't afford to marry." He gestured to them. "Maybe he's an orphan and has to make his way in the world and works too hard to take time to engage in politics or other community agencies that influence his town." He paused and looked into their upturned faces. "But if God's Word is in his heart, and he listens to his Father's voice and obeys, boys, and stands up for the rights of women and children—that's a man of character."

Behind him someone applauded. "Well said." The pastor and his wife grinned, as did Mrs. Labron, who wore an expression of regret.

What was Juliana's friend regretful of?

Although it was almost summer, a damp chill accompanied Juliana as she'd ridden her Victor's Lady's Safety bicycle to work, on her first day back. Now inside, inhaling the mingled scents of books, inkprint, and lemon oil should have brought a sense of normalcy to her life. Instead, it seemed as though she'd stepped aboard a ship that was listing and about to sink. She rubbed her throat where the rope burns still chafed her and shivered. No wonder Rebecca Hart had seemed so aloof at times.

Seated in the back workroom, Juliana opened crates of books with one of the newly hired library interns from Michigan Normal School.

Graham Arsenault, who'd grown up in the area, lifted and displayed a copy of *The Picture of Dorian Gray.* "I read the original magazine version and I've heard the editors deleted some of the, er…"

"More objectionable material?" Juliana arched an eyebrow at him. Claudette had been waiting on this book.

"Yes." He laughed. "My mother would be shocked, but your sister would love it—Claudette always enjoyed those frightful Gothic stories, if I remember right."

"You do recall correctly. Let's set it aside for her." *Maybe Claudette will read it to Richard and the lumberjacks at the camp.* She drew in a slow steadying breath and then exhaled.

Gracie popped her head in. "Graham, do you mind covering the front desk?"

"Be happy to."

He slipped out, and Gracie sat down across from her at the long rectangular table, covered with boxes and new books.

"Are you feeling better?"

"I am." Other than wishing she could just be alone.

"Did you see that The Pines Restaurant has opened?"

"Has it?" Excitement skittered through her shooing her crankiness away. "It's so beautiful, isn't it?" With its wide majestic porch, fancy gingerbread trim and glossy burgundy shutters, it stood out from the older establishments.

"I can't help wondering if it's as fancy inside as it is outside." Gracie heaved a sigh. "I've never gotten to eat at any of the restaurants in town."

"Really?"

Gracie never complained. But now the girl's eyes glittered with unshed tears.

Juliana reached across the table and squeezed her friend's hand. "If I could, I'd take you to all of them."

"Have you been in any?"

"Only a few of the older ones from before..." When her father had been alive.

Gracie's frown vanished and she clapped her hands together. "What do you think of our new helpers?"

"We sure need those young men, with all the tourists." Summer vacationers swelled the number of visitors to their library. Thank goodness the students had already been contracted, prior to the horrible attack. Her skin yet crawled at the thought of that man's hands around her neck. Poor Rebecca—how had she born being hung from a tree, pretending to have fainted, thrown in a river and left to drown? But Garrett and Richard had rescued her. She rubbed her arms as a chill coursed up them.

"And some of the lumberjacks and their families are beginning to move up to the area. Your Mr. Christy brought in three men this morning to get their library cards. Have you seen him?"

"No." Nor did she want to. The incident should have drawn her closer to the lumberjack, but she'd not gotten over her nightmares—that included him—and had a terrible one the night before. Her thoughts were irrational. The man had saved her, she should be grateful. The woman she'd been before the attack would have thrilled, perhaps swooned over the idea of him rescuing her. But now, it seemed as though God was preparing her for another chapter in her life. Unfinished business in her life needed to be addressed. She'd thought Richard might be that new beginning, but gazing down at her hands, still lightly wrapped in gauze, she couldn't help wondering if she wasn't being punished for her vanity and silliness. And with her suspicions that Claudette and Richard may hold affection for one another, Juliana wanted to step out of the way.

Gracie stood. "Well, I'm going back out. And when you're done hiding, please join us."

Juliana opened her mouth to protest but couldn't find her voice. It was true. She was secreting herself away from the patrons. One in particular.

An hour later, Juliana emerged from the workroom. Her steadfast assistant waved from behind the counter.

"He's back!" Gracie adjusted her waistband and then carefully rearranged the folds of her white cotton blouse so that they lay evenly.

"Hmmm?" Juliana removed two Herman Melville books from the returns stack on a nearby cart and set them atop the oak counter. *Such a shame so few read Melville's works any more—but at least someone had.* "Who is back?"

Gracie cupped her hands around her mouth and whispered in Juliana's ear. "James Yost has returned. I saw him at Labrons' store yesterday, and he asked me tell you he'd be by today. Sorry, but I forgot until I saw him just now."

Oh no. The beer baron, again. Here. And she'd have to thank him for his charity. She should do so—but why didn't she want to? "Hadn't he gone back to Milwaukee?" If he waylaid her again and claimed he wanted to discuss Dewey's system—at length—she might just call his bluff. Maybe the man truly did wish to discuss library science with her, but she doubted his motives were purely for the motivation to organize his new library in Milwaukee.

Just then, the man emerged from the nonfiction aisle and walked toward them carrying an ebony-headed cane. His black leather shoes gleamed and a bowler was tucked under his arm. He smiled in their direction.

"Let me take the cart and put the returns away." Gracie's winsome features settled into a professional mask as she grabbed the bar of the book cart and pulled it away from behind the counter.

When Gracie immediately veered in the direction of Mr. Yost, Juliana drew in a long breath. Sure enough, James Yost immediately engaged her assistant in conversation, periodically glancing in Juliana's direction. The man was persistent, she'd give him that much. And she should thank him for the supplies he'd sent out. But it was rather presumptuous of him to send them as well as implying they required his charity, which didn't sit well with her. She could provide for her own family, and would.

"Ma'am, do ya have a minute?" Richard Christy's deep voice startled her and she jumped.

Her hands flew from the books they rested on. "How can I help you?"

A low chuckle rumbled from his chest. For some reason that irritated her.

He was the one who had helped her so why should he frighten her now? He'd saved her. Her hands began to shake, remembering the feel of his arms around her as he'd carried her.

"Ya sure do look pretty, Juliana, that is Miss Beauchamps."

He'd called her Juliana. But he'd also taken to calling her sister Claudette. Why did Richard Christy cause such confusion in her? She should avoid him, but she couldn't do so while she was at work. She daren't look up into his handsome face. But she wanted so badly to look into those dark eyes. She drew in a slow breath. With effort, she tried to swallow the knot that formed in her throat every time the lumberjack came by. An unbidden image surfaced of him in bare feet, his pants rolled up, and his undershirt stretched taut over his muscles. She wanted to shoo the thought away but it persisted.

"Thank you." She tugged at the curls around her face.

"I reckon ya might not think a lumberjack enjoys poetry, but I do." His husky voice drew her attention as he leaned in so close that she could see the amber flecks in his dark brown eyes. "I just don't want anyone else seein' me with this book—especially since I think it's written for ladies."

He clutched one of her favorite poet's books. She recognized the tome, despite his broad hand covering Elizabeth Barrett Browning's name.

Blinking up at him, she combatted the conflicting desires to lean in a little closer, drawn by the handsome man, or to fuss at him for his vanity. *Too proud a many woodsman to be seen with a poetry book in his hand.* She'd just been literally burned because of her own prideful behavior, wanting to see her new gown. Her wandering thoughts of Richard's muscular legs well in check, now, she ground out her question, "And I am to do what about this dilemma of yours?"

He puffed out his cheeks and straightened. "I thought we were gettin' to be friends."

The man had rescued her from what would have been certain death. He'd invited her to The Lumberjacks' Ball. And he thought of them as mere friends? She stared at him, speechless. Or was this the "friend speech" and he was distancing himself so he could pursue the lovelier sister? And why did she care if he did—didn't her mixed up feelings tell her that he'd brought fear into her life?

"And I wondered…"

He sure had some nerve. "Oh. You want me to check them out for you."

Richard grinned, and though it would seem he couldn't possibly be any more appealing than he was, that smile sent a current through her.

"I'm sorry, Mr. Christy, but it is against library policy for me to check out a book for a patron." She pressed her lips together in a prim smirk.

When his face fell, she almost felt bad. But it was true—she couldn't simply check out books because someone was afraid to be seen with a book of love poems by a prominent female author.

Nearby, someone cleared his throat. As Mr. Yost left Gracie's side, he cocked his head and caught Juliana's attention. He adjusted the lapels of his expensive tailored-to-perfection linen jacket, worn with pleated and cuffed linen trousers. Then he strode toward the desk, knocking his elbow into Richard in the process—an act that appeared deliberate.

The lumberjack glared down at the not-much-shorter man. "Wait your turn in line, buddy." He narrowed his eyes.

The other man shrugged and grinned at Juliana. "Must I wait, Miss Beauchamps?"

"Not at all, Mr. Yost." She gave him a tight smile. "I believe Mr. Christy is unable to complete his library request..."

"At this time," he completed for her. Then he had the audacity to wink.

She directed her gaze to Mr. Yost and affected an especially sweet tone of voice. "And thank you for the supplies you sent out, sir—the orphans who visit with us were especially touched by your generosity."

Richard stretched his broad shoulders back and glared down at the beer baron. "You did that?"

Yost shrugged. "It was nothing. I was glad to help."

"Can see ya don't need me here." With that, the lumberjack turned away from them.

After Richard had taken five long strides away, Mr. Yost sighed. "That buffoon hasn't been bothering you, has he?"

That is no buffoon, but the new owner of a lumber camp who will be in charge of a hundred men. She bit back the desire to tell him that of all the men in town, it was he, himself, who bothered her most. Oh, if only she didn't feel so confused about Richard.

"How can I assist you?"

"I would like to invite you and your assistant to dinner tonight at The Pines. I'd love to discuss the Dewey decimal system with you."

Gracie edged the book cart closer, her gaze fixed on them, eyes wide. Juliana wanted to say "no", but seeing the longing in her assistant's eyes, she nodded.

"Perhaps. But, being a resident of the orphanage, Gracie will need to secure permission from Sister Mary Lou in order to accompany us."

"Let's ask that sweet nun. I see her sitting in the corner with three of her little charges." His charming smile could persuade almost anyone, including Sister Mary Lou, and James Yost likely knew it. His comment bothered her nonetheless.

Why wouldn't he have simply suggested that they go alone? He couldn't consider Gracie an appropriate chaperone.

His face momentarily contorted. "I would enjoy a solitary dinner with you, Miss Beauchamps, to discuss library organization systems in depth, but I fear the library board would frown upon it. I do believe your apprentice can help us make our companionship much more palatable to the trustees. Don't you agree?"

"True." She'd about had her fill of the board members, who'd deigned to withhold her pay until she returned to work. *Talk about Christian charity or the lack of it.* All of those men were regular churchgoers, but Janet Labron shared that her husband was the only man present at the meeting who'd suggested they continue to pay her while she recovered.

But what could she do? She'd worked so hard for so long.

Rest in me. Trust me. The almost audible voice made Juliana jump and she almost spilled the inkwell atop the counter. But when she scanned the room, her eyes settled on Richard—her own Bon Jean come to life and her heart skipped a beat. Standing between two rows of bookcases, his dark head bowed over the book of sonnets, he resembled the giant lumberjack of her childhood daydreams.

Someone cleared his throat loudly. Juliana cringed, anticipating her nemesis.

Mr. Hatchens stepped alongside her and she wished she could run away. "I might ask you a penny for your thoughts, Miss Beauchamps, but it's clear that shanty boy is distracting you."

"No, sir. I'm just..." Juliana drew in a deep breath, catching the musty smell of the trustee's suit. "I'm surprised that our library's Bon Jean enjoys poetry." The moment the words were out of her mouth, she willed them back in, again, and resisted the urge to press her fingertips to her offending lips. She shouldn't have pointed out where Richard was standing and she shouldn't have referred to him as their Bon Jean.

The board member smirked. "Didn't realize we had children's poetry in that section, Miss Beauchamps. I doubt that gargantuan reads the great poets, like Wadsworth. So don't trouble yourself over his behavior. Leave that to me. We can rein him in."

Oh no. What did that mean? Before she could form a cohesive protest, Mr. Hatchens pulled out a notepad and a pencil, scribbled something down, and sped toward the door.

Chapter 7

The previous evening, after spending dinner with Mr. Yost, resulted in a splitting headache and a night's worth of fitful sleep. When she'd not felt any better in the morning, she'd taken the carriage to work, unsure she could manage her bicycle. The day, at the library, hadn't gone much better as Richard hadn't visited the library. Driving home from work, Juliana slowed their bay gelding to a walk, taking in the beauty of the lush forest near her home. If she turned the carriage to the right, she could go to the Christy's lumber camp. Hesitating, the horse must have sensed her indecision for he neighed and shook his head, attempting to pull to the left. She slapped the reins and they continued on toward home. She glimpsed a flash of sapphire blue through the break in the trees. Lake Michigan beckoned to her to come take a dip in the water. And she might—later.

Four cabins surrounded the main house, two on either side, all unoccupied, even though Papa had built them to hold his *"grand hommes,"* as he liked to call her big older brothers. She'd not been able to make any repairs to them since Papa died. But Juliana would not worry about that right now. She just needed to get home and get dinner on. Unless, tonight, again, Claudette fried fish brought by Richard Christy. What did the two talk about? Claudette never shared, which rankled Juliana. She always told her younger sister about her own day, especially since Claudette had experienced a bad episode the previous winter and had become more isolated.

Soon Juliana arrived home and had taken care of the horse and carriage. Claudette stepped down from the porch, where she'd been rocking. "I have whitefish for tonight."

Juliana cocked an eyebrow. "Let me guess. Mr. Christy brought them?"

Sunlight haloed her sister's golden hair. "He did, indeed, and he told Mother and me all about the new ladies he's interviewed for the camp cook jobs."

"Have his prospects improved?" She pulled the crystal-headed hatpins free from her straw boater and removed it as they walked to the house.

Laughing, her sister grasped her hand and swung it. "I believe Richard's luck is about to change."

Mother met them at the door and cast Claudette a cautionary look. "We'll discuss things later. But first I want to bring your sister up to date on some of the changes we might have around here."

Fiddling with her hat, Juliana accidentally poked her finger with one of her hatpins. "Ow!" She pressed the pierced finger to her lips.

As she took a step back down the porch, about to go to the pump, her mother gently grasped her shoulder. "I've already pumped water and hauled it—enough for a hot bath heating on the stove—so come on inside and let's clean that up."

This was the mother of her youth. The mother she'd thought she'd lost to rheumatism after her father's death. Was she back to stay?

Later, after a splendid dinner, Mother cleared the table and then returned with rhubarb pie and cut it into generous slices.

Tugging at her collar, Claudette fixed Juliana with a mysterious look. "You know, someday I may be well and you may again find someone you'd wish to marry."

And might you be interested in marrying Richard? Juliana clamped her mouth shut, sure the green-eyed monster inhabiting her body would leap out.

Mother returned to the stove and then brought coffee back for them and three mugs. "I went into town today and everyone says James Yost must be interested in you."

Juliana cringed. She'd suffered enough gossip for a lifetime. "Oh? And how did you get there, Mother, since I had the carriage?"

"Never you mind—but Richard gave me a ride." Now her mother was calling him by his Christian name? "And you are changing the subject, which is James Yost."

Claudette poured cream into each of their mugs. "How did your dinner go last night?"

Grabbing the sugar bowl and, eyeing her sister, Juliana proceeded to pluck out four cubes, instead of using the tongs. She tossed them in her coffee, the satisfying "plunk" making her grin.

Mother chuckled. "He must have gotten under your skin. You didn't say much when you came home."

With a groan, Juliana stirred her coffee. "James Yost grates on my nerves." Last night the man seemed jumpy, for some reason, which had ratcheted up her anxiety level.

Claudette laughed. "With all of his money, I imagine a great many women could overlook a little edginess."

Juliana shook her head. "There is something so officious about him. He kept talking about setting up and maintaining order in his new library in Milwaukee. And how many books he planned for the private library in his mansion—and how they all must be in perfect order!"

"Of course men prefer order in their households. Think of your father." Mother's eyes filmed over.

"He's not like Papa." Not at all. Salt of the earth didn't apply to the beer baron. "Mr. Yost kept questioning me about Dewey's system…"

"And what else?" Claudette's eyes lit up. Her poor sister needed to get out more often, if she was this starved for gossip.

"Well, he'd alternate his library questions with compliments about my appearance." She flushed remembering the comment that her eyes were like "rare sapphires."

"Compliments?" Mother arched one eyebrow.

Juliana raised her coffee cup and drank for a long time, hoping the two would leave her be. "He said nice things to Gracie, too." Which was very kind of him to not leave her assistant out of the conversation.

Her sister patted a stray curl on her forehead back into place. "He's very handsome—I met him once at Labrons' store."

Mother nodded. "Very good-looking, and I've never seen a more dapper gentleman in these parts."

"I just keep feeling like he wants something from me that is unsavory." Even though he'd never made any inappropriate overtures toward her. In fact, he'd always been extremely polite.

Holding her forkful of pie mid-air, Mother hesitated. "Maybe that isn't it—maybe it's because the man is a widower."

Heat seared her neck and cheeks. She'd wondered the same thing. Had the intimacies between a man and a woman in marriage caused him to give her such strange, searching looks? "Maybe that's why he seems so…well…intense in his concentration on a subject or a person. Passionate. Perhaps, having been married—"

Mother held up her palm.

When Claudette's eyes grew wide, Juliana added, "Not that those activities, blessed by God, are anything bad."

Her mother laughed. "I wouldn't have born all those children if they had been."

Both Claudette and Juliana stifled a gasp but then joined her in chuckling.

"Even if he does look at you in that…married way…he's so charming." After lifting her fork and taking a bite, Claudette grinned around a mouthful of rhubarb pie.

"Yes, and handsome and wealthy as you mentioned." Was Mother worrying about Juliana?

Juliana should be thrilled by his attention at the library and in the community, but an inner voice cautioned her. Papa would have said she was discerning and he'd have told her to avoid him, which she'd tried to do.

"I think Aleksantari was too young to marry you, Juliana." Her mother sipped her coffee.

Alek? They were speaking of Yost, not her former beau.

"You must forgive him."

"I have forgiven." Hadn't she? She clenched her teeth. "Besides, he wasn't a young lad—he was over twenty."

Claudette rolled her eyes. "Maybe immature is a better word than young."

"He was childish—not that I look back and waste time considering." Perhaps that wasn't true.

Her sister gave her a knowing look. "Right."

Juliana shrugged. "Self-centered and self-absorbed might have described him back then." Yost, too, seemed single-minded. In this case, the beer baron seemed obsessed with libraries.

"Wonder how Alek likes Milwaukee." Claudette wiped a crumb from the corner of her mouth.

"Milwaukee? He was in the mines." And how did her sister know?

"I heard he's in Milwaukee now, too." Mother finished her last bite of pie.

Juliana didn't care where her old beau was. All she knew was she needed to support her mother and sister the best she could. Her brothers were certainly of no help.

"Juliana, we've heard from Pauline." Her mother lifted her cup, the dark circles under her eyes emphasized by the white porcelain.

Her brother's widow hadn't been to St. Ignace in years.

Claudette chewed her lower lip. "Um hum. She wrote."

Juliana stood and took the dishes to the sink, awaiting an explanation. She swiveled around and found Claudette frowning.

"Pauline is bringing the children back here to live." Claudette's gaze held a challenge. "Here. With us."

Mother stared at her lap. "Her father died."

A wave of dizziness swept over Juliana. "Here? Why not remain in his home?"

"She said his debts will take his estate and she has nowhere else to go." Mother met her eyes with that iron-willed gaze of hers that allowed no discussion.

Oh no. Not just one more mouth to feed but four. She knew she should be happy to see her nieces and nephew, and have more family nearby but... *How Lord? How am I to do this?*

Oversleeping had cost her the ten extra minutes Juliana needed to change out of her bicycling costume and into her normal clothes for work. If only the social mores and strictures of society didn't impinge on her physical freedom. Then she'd not have to concern herself with the delay of changing clothes. Why, in some places, women wore pantaloons to all manner of functions. Last summer, Juliana had even spied a tourist from Chicago sporting chartreuse silk bloomers to the Independence Day picnic basket auction. That was quite a sight. She grinned as she cycled as fast as she could toward the back of the library and slid her bike into the stand, wondering what Mr. Hatchens would say if Juliana wore such a getup to work. But then, a stiff breeze from the harbor made her shiver and she imagined what her work clothes, crammed in her rucksack, would look like after she pulled them out. She hurried toward the back door, which Gracie held open for her.

"Hurry! Mr. Hatchens is already walking up the street."

"Oh no!" But if the board hadn't required her to represent the library at Mrs. Jeffries' event, she wouldn't have been up half the night preparing. She'd assembled and cleaned the jewelry, stockings, dress shoes, and hair accessories she'd need to go with her ensemble. What did they mean by asking her at the last minute, anyway? Those men—surely they didn't expect her to show up in her work clothes.

Gracie shoved Juliana past her and toward the ladies room. Once inside, she fumbled with her rucksack and finally emptied it, her dark skirt falling to the floor. She snatched it up and brushed it off. Thankfully, the janitor had done a good cleaning the night before. She pulled off her bicycling trousers and slipped into the skirt then fumbled in the bottom of her bag, for her belt. No belt. She tucked her blouse into the skirt. Juliana felt for her smaller bag with her necklace from Papa and earrings, her best stockings, her shiny church shoes, and the seven crystal studded tortoiseshell combs she needed to secure all her hair. Everything else was there but her belt.

Her assistant popped her head in. "Hurry! He's asking for you."

After coiling her braid up into a demure bun, Juliana pushed the tendrils around her face back into her hairline. No hair dare be out of place when Hatchens entered the library to spy. She splashed a little water from the pitcher into her hands and onto her face and then dabbed it dry. *Dear Lord, please let him be reasonable today. Don't let him find anything out of order. And Lord, I hope it is your will I keep my job because I sure need it.*

"That wasn't Miss Beauchamps I saw scuttling into the back entrance just now, was it?" Mr. Hatchen's voice held a sneer.

When she rounded the corner to her desk, the man was actually leaning over it, rifling through her neatly stacked cards.

"Please cease your disruption." Juliana scowled as she hurried to stop him from messing up her alphabetical arrangement of overdue books.

"What?" His attempt to assume an air of innocence failed and a guilty wash of red touched his cheekbones.

"Mr. Hatchens." Gracie's honey-sweet voice was surely meant to distract him. The seventeen-year-old beauty rocked back and forth, her hands clutched demurely at her waist. "Now, sir, you know better than to interfere with order here in the library."

"What order?" he blustered. He gestured to where piles of books cluttered the center of a circle edged with children's books.

"Those picture books are set out for the orphan's group." Juliana narrowed her eyes at him. Truth be told, she'd had enough of his interference. There had to be someone on the board who could help her.

"Did the trustees approve this group to be ongoing?" He smirked. "I've asked them to discontinue it. And I want that lumberjack fellow to stay away from the children."

Juliana pushed her now-messy stack of cards aside and drew in a steadying breath. "You well know that when I was hired, this was one of our first library programs offered." And Richard had done nothing wrong.

He sniffed and averted his gaze.

"Oh, I forgot. You weren't on the board then, were you?" She ground out these last words despite the voice in her head screaming that she should be buttering this man up—not annoying him.

"Of course he wasn't, Miss Juliana." Gracie batted her lashes and leaned in toward the man. "He and his lovely family only moved here right when I arrived at the orphanage three years ago. And Mrs. Hatchens is the sweetest lady."

He backed away from her. "You're an orphan?" He might have asked if Gracie was a leper.

The color drained from the girl's face. "Why, yes, sir, you signed for me to volunteer here."

He waved a hand at her as though whisking away a fly.

"Excuse me, Miss Juliana." Gracie spun on her heel and headed toward the far stacks.

No matter that her temper was hot as a poker left in the fire too long, Juliana needed this job. She had to regain control.

The double doors into the library swung open, allowing light to create a path on the crimson and gold wool rug that covered the planked floors. James Yost entered, and a sandy-haired young man accompanied him, clutching a notebook. Right behind them, Richard Christy slipped in and disappeared behind a row of books, ending her brief hope of his rescue.

The obnoxious trustee swiveled to face them. "Good morning, gentlemen. How can I help you?"

Mr. Yost's pale eyes widened and he cocked his head to the side. "I believe that is Miss Beauchamps' duty, sir, to assist patrons."

"I'm a Library Board member, and I consider it my responsibility…"

"Splendid. A man who owns his responsibilities. I believe we have much to discuss." Mr. Yost took the board member by his elbow, and led him over to the alcove by the entrance.

What is that all about?

Richard Christy ambled out of the fiction section, toward the counter, and passed a copy of *Aurora Leigh*, Book One in Elizabeth Barrett Browning's series, to her.

"You want to read this?" She scarce could believe it.

When his dark eyes met hers and he grinned, her heart hitched up into her throat and Juliana simply stared back at him, grasping the book to her chest.

"Can ya check that back in for me, Miss Beauchamps, please?" His impertinent wink brought her back to her senses.

"Back in?"

"Yes, Miss Gracie checked it out for me." He smiled, his teeth gleaming beneath his beard.

"She didn't…" Gracie wouldn't have jeopardized her position as library assistant. "That is, did you check this out in your name?"

"Yes, ma'am." He pulled himself up to his full height. "And I enjoyed it right well."

"You read it all?" She'd not seen much of him since the night he'd found her at The Pines with Mr. Yost. Did he know she'd seen him duck in and then right back out of the new restaurant? And she'd seen his scowl, too, when the hostess pointed out the dress code. Apparently Paul Bon Jean was not welcome in the newest restaurant where pristine linen table cloths, polished silverware, and brilliant crystal chandeliers might clash with faded red-and-black checked flannel.

"I read it every night." He ran a finger over his full lower lip. What would it feel like to kiss those lips? Would his beard tickle?

Stop those thoughts right now!

"Made me feel right lonely, though."

"Isn't it less lonely out there, now that the lumberjacks are trickling into camp?" She bit her lower lip as Mr. Hatchens turned from Mr. Yost and observed her. She dare not continue to engage in personal conversation.

"Dont'cha want to know what brings me back into town?" An ebony curl fell across the man's brow as he leaned in so close that she could smell the fresh scent of pine on him.

Juliana swallowed but couldn't utter a word. Dare she hope? Had he come to town to see her? Why couldn't she get him off her mind?

He straightened and adjusted his suspenders. "I'm fixin' to interview that doc for the camp."

She puffed out a breath. "A physician?"

"Not just any physician—the one who helped you." Richard grinned and tugged on his suspenders.

"Oh." So her Bon Jean lookalike wasn't there for her.

"And not full time, mind ya, but part of the time."

"I see." She didn't.

"Dr. Adams-Payne came up from downstate to work in Newberry, but he's willin' to come out to my camp once or twice a month."

She tried to make her mouth work. "That's splendid," finally came out.

He turned to look at the two men in the alcove, their heads close together, before directing his attention back to her. "Don't reckon this is any of my business, but what's Hatchens got against you, Miss Beauchamps?"

"Nothing." My, that came out too quickly and too loudly. Both gentlemen looked in their direction. She quickly made motions of stamping Richard's book back in and filing his card.

Jo Christy came through the front door and made a beeline to her brother. She took his arm. "You have a lot of work to do today. Cordelia sent me to fetch you."

Richard's cheekbones flushed above his beard. He gestured toward Juliana. "Ain't ya gonna at least say hello to Miss Beauchamps while yer here, ya bossy sister?"

Making a silly face, Jo stretched up on her tiptoes toward her brother and wagged a finger at him. "What's a big sister for, if not to boss the likes of a younger brother around?"

Juliana looked between the two. Jo wasn't older. But she must be. She just said she was.

The auburn-haired beauty smiled at Juliana. "Good to see you, Juliana. And I bet you know why I immediately sought my baby brother out here."

Baby brother? A sinking feeling started in Juliana's gut. Had she misheard Garrett Christy at Rebecca's shop? She'd thought he'd said Richard was the elder brother. "He loves to read, doesn't he?" she croaked. Rebecca had told her that Josephine was twenty-five.

"It would seem so."

Josephine shook her head. "Can you believe such a great big hairy fellow was a skinny little boy?" She held out her hand to waist height between her and her brother.

"Aw, Sis. Stop it." Richard rolled his eyes like an annoyed young lad would.

The woman's tinkling laughter followed her as she waved and pulled Richard toward the door. He raised his hand in a brief wave before they disappeared out into the sunlit day.

Appearances could be deceiving. Juliana plunked down on her stool, behind the desk, and stared around the library. This had become her world after Aleksanteri had left and never sent for her. After Papa made sure she had a livelihood when no other man came to call on her. How old was Richard anyway? There had been a twenty-six year age difference between her eldest brother, Gerard, and Claudette. The oldest he could be was twenty four. Claudette's age. And the youngest? She didn't even want to think about it. Just like she didn't want to consider that her mother, at seventy, may never see either of her post-Civil War daughters wed. Had she and Papa been trying for replacement sons, like her older brothers insisted? Too bad the two youngest of the surviving brothers had thought so, resented their younger sisters, and left for the military as soon as they could.

Gracie sidled up to Juliana. "Have our contracts come in yet?"

Chapter 8

All afternoon, Richard assisted his father and brother and the hired men in setting up Cordelia's Inn for the grand opening for the community. He'd need a good bath before changing into his fancy duds for the dinner that night.

"I wanted to let the people of St. Ignace know how happy I am to be here." Cordelia stood at the entrance to the main dining room, which could seat nearly seventy people. She gazed from one end to another, a smile of satisfaction fixed on her face.

Richard had never seen so much china, silver, and crystal in one place at the same time. Well, maybe at The Pines, but he'd not gotten far enough into the establishment to appreciate it. He had, however, that night, gotten a good look at old Yost making cow eyes at Juliana. She'd be better off with him. If she married the beer baron, he'd take care of the Beauchamps family. Yost was a generous man, from what all the Milwaukee newspapers said about him—and Richard had paid a pretty penny to buy the periodicals up and scour them through for any hint of scandal. None.

Jo pinched his arm and laughed. "You're deep in thought."

He growled at her and she laughed.

"Well little brother, pretty soon, I bet there'll be electric lights in this inn. Wouldn't that be something?"

"Sure would." What other changes would electricity bring? The world was changing. His thoughts went back to Hatchens. Maybe that was the trustee's problem. Women in Michigan were a hard-working bunch—had to be—but

Hatchens wanted to keep them as they'd been earlier in the century. But he was progressive in other ways. Charles Labron had shared that when electricity did come in, Hatchens wanted his house to be one of the first with it. He'd even considered buying an electrical generator, but didn't when he realized the noise it would make and didn't want his wife disturbed. And in teaching Sunday School for the last few weeks, Richard had heard Atlas Hatchens make only positive comments about his father, including the man's deep love and respect for his wife.

The scents of roasting beef, potatoes, and sweet apples mingled with coffee and the deeper scent of chocolate and cinnamon, and pulled Richard from his thoughts. His stomach began to growl. "The smell of all that good food you're fixin' in the kitchen is gonna kill me if I don't have some soon."

A smile twitched on Jo's lips. "Maybe I need to tell Juliana good cooking is the way to your heart then, and not poetry?"

He tried to force a scowl, but they both laughed. His sister always could read him like a book.

Tom Jeffries crept up behind Jo, an index finger placed to his lips. Then he poked Jo in her sides and she shrieked and swiveled around.

"Why you!" She swatted at him but her fiancé grabbed her hands.

"You're needed in the kitchen, my love." Tom kissed Jo's forehead and then grasped her hand and led her away.

The light from the hallway dimmed as a broad-shouldered man filled the entryway. "Pa?"

In three strides, his father was beside him and pulled him into a brief bear hug and then hammered him on his shoulders. "Ya ain't gettin' weak livin' up here, are ya?"

"No, sir." He'd not tell him he struck him on a sore spot.

"And ya ain't jumpin' into any more fires, are ya?" Pa laughed but when he gave him another quick hug, Richard knew his father had been scared for him.

"No, sir. No more fires." And no more Peevey. Since getting right with God, Richard had been troubled that the wicked man likely burned in an eternal hellfire. But there was nothing to be done for it now. Other than to work with boys at Sunday School and instill in them the need for wisdom, especially as laid down in Proverbs, fourth chapter, which he'd be teaching on this week. Maybe he'd reach a boy, who like Peevey went home to an alcoholic abusive father and had no one to instill God's Word in him.

"I'm glad." His father scanned the room and then waved to the inn's owner.

Cordelia Jeffries left the table she'd been examining, and joined them. "So good to see you, Mr. Christy. And I assume my sister is here somewhere?"

"She sure is. Said somethin' about wantin' to lay her gown out real quick so it don't wrinkle."

Mrs. Jeffries dipped her chin in acknowledgement.

"Cordelia, you've got a beautiful place here." Pa grinned, as he eyed the banquet room. "You're tempting me to take up permanent residence."

Mrs. Jeffries fussed with her lacy collar. "Irene knows you are both welcome to live at the inn, until you figure out what direction your new life should take."

He still couldn't believe Pa was marrying Irene, who also happened to be Tom Jeffries' aunt. The Christy family was about to get all mixed together with the Jeffries. Jo's mother-in-law would end up being her aunt by marriage and her stepmother, too. The handsome woman seemed a good fit for Pa, though, and up to the challenge of dealing with all the menfolk. Tonight Irene and Pa were going to advise him on the hiring for the camp. Although Richard had some ideas, it was, after all, Pa's money he was putting up.

"I'm so glad you could be here for our very first event." Mrs. Jeffries reminded him of a schoolgirl, with the way she clapped her hands together. Juliana was like that, too, or had been before the fire. He missed that about her—she didn't seem excited about things like before. But maybe that would return.

He wasn't worthy of her, regardless. Who was he kidding? He was a lumberjack and she was an educated young woman.

Pa elbowed him. "You all right, son?"

"Yeah. A little tired."

The inn owner beamed. "I've kept him busy."

Richard laughed. "Tom would say your comment was an understatement."

"Tom would wax eloquent as to all your physical efforts today on my behalf, I'm sure. He'd even make your sweating and hoisting furniture around sound poetic." She smiled. "Come, let me show you who is sitting where."

Richard followed them past white linen-covered tables, each topped by bouquets of garden flowers. The scent in the room reminded him of Juliana's perfume. He sneezed. He scanned the vases and soon found the culprits—lilacs in several of the larger bouquets. The powerful perfume didn't agree with him. "Um, Mrs. Jeffries, I reckon you may have forgotten, but I get a bad case of sneezing fits when lilacs are around."

Her mouth formed an "O". "I'm so sorry. I forgot. Let me have those removed." She waved at one of the wait staff. "Please remove all the lilacs from the bouquets."

"Sure thing, Mrs. Jeffries." The slim blond man frowned. "But could I give them to my sister? She loves them."

"Fine, but remove them from the building. You have permission to store them in Garrett's workshop outside."

Richard would stay away from there. "Yes, ma'am."

After Richard sneezed three times in succession, Pa directed him toward the exit. "Go get some fresh air, son."

"Yes, sir."

"First, let me show him where you'll be seated for tonight." Mrs. Jeffries gestured to the longest table. "We'll be putting the Library Trustees there, in the back. They plan to discuss business as well as enjoy the meal."

Here was an opportunity. Richard cleared his throat. "Ma'am, do you think we could be seated near them?"

"I'd planned to seat you in a more open area closer to the kitchen at the front." She shrugged. "I don't know why we couldn't place you near the back. Would that be all right with you, Mr. Christy?"

Pa cast him a quizzical look and Richard waggled his eyebrows back. They'd had this form of silent communication the past several years when either had gotten an idea but didn't want to discuss their notions in front of anyone. "Fine by me. Now you go on, boy—get outta here before yer eyes swell up."

"Yes, sir."

As Richard left the building, he passed several more waiters who were carrying in baskets of rolls, breads, and muffins and fancy bowls filled with butter pressed into shapes. He let out a low whistle. This was going to be quite a night. The whole shebang was top notch.

An idea flashed through his mind. How long would it take to have his beard shaved off, like his brother had done? Would that draw Miss Beauchamps attention any further? Maybe if he didn't look so much like a green shanty boy, then she'd actually look into his eyes instead of away from him all the time—as she had done since the fire. Like she had at the restaurant. He knew she'd seen him, but she didn't even acknowledge him. She could have at least done that little half-wave that ladies do when they notice a friend but are too busy to greet them. Maybe he wouldn't make her so nervous if he weren't so hairy. Her hands always seemed to tremble within minutes of them talking. He tugged at his beard.

He headed off to the barber, who soon accomplished a miracle, removing his beard more quickly than Richard thought possible. Of course everyone would still know who he was since he was the tallest man in town, but if he was sitting down, maybe not. That meant he had to get to the banquet before the librarian and the trustees showed up.

He rubbed his hand along his smooth jaw. Should have done this long ago.

Won't Juliana be surprised?

Sister Mary Lou had removed as much of the old-fashioned bustle as she could from Juliana's gown. She, Gracie, and Juliana huddled in the nun's room. "I've simplified the skirt."

She held the dress aloft, but it still appeared dreadfully out of date. "Thank you, Sister Mary Lou."

The board had to know that her salary, which was much less than a man was generally offered for the same position, wouldn't attire her in all the latest fashion. Not that it mattered, since she was to be there at the opening of the inn's banquet hall to represent the library and not be the belle of some ball. She'd hoped to finally break free of the gossip over Alek's abandonment of her. Hoped to be dressed in her gorgeous gown, on the arm of the handsomest lumberjack. But if Richard Christy knew how old she was, would he even take her to The Lumberjacks' Ball? She frowned. And wouldn't tongues wag even more if he ended up being a half dozen years or more younger than she was?

The nun ran a hand along her jawline, watching Gracie fasten the last button on Juliana's remade gown.

The pretty girl rotated slowly, giving them the full effect. "That length of tulle you added underneath has made my dress plenty long enough."

"With your hair up like that, Gracie, you do look all grown up!" Sister Mary Lou wiped a tear from her eyes, which were rimmed underneath with dark rings. Their friend needed rest. And a break from all of her responsibilities. And here she'd done more work, hastily fixing both Gracie's and Juliana's dresses.

"I should have worn my gown made for the ball." Juliana chewed her lower lip.

"Oh no, dear. That dress is too special for this occasion. Save that for the Lumberjacks' Ball." Sister Mary Lou patted her on the arm. "Now get changed. We've got work to do."

Soon, fully gowned, bejeweled, and mincing in their best shoes, Juliana and Gracie linked arms and headed down the street toward the inn, garnering appreciative glances as they went. With her blonde hair upswept, Gracie looked like a princess. Juliana's dark tresses were swirled around her head in a fashionable style even if her dress was out of mode. And her pearls, once worn by Papa's mother, and passed to her as the eldest daughter, made Juliana feel special—cherished as though Papa was right there with her. She blinked away the moisture in her eyes as she and Gracie ascended the black-painted steps up into the inn.

On the wide porch, surrounding the front of the inn, a small group of library board members clustered. They were probably waiting for Mr. Hatchens to join them before entering. And if they were all here, why was she—the head librarian—needed for this event? She cringed, wondering if one of them would motion her over and request that she sit with them. But they all ignored Juliana and Gracie. Relief coursed through her.

Her assistant suddenly clutched Juliana's arm harder. "This is the most exciting thing I've done in my life."

Juliana's most thrilling day was when she'd become engaged to Aleksanteri. But that was many years ago. And then she'd had to change her dream. She'd put aside her plans to live in the Puumala's lumber camp, where she'd be cooking and raising a half dozen children, and had headed off to school. She chased the memory away as she disengaged Gracie's arm from hers and squeezed her hand gently. "I pray you make wonderful memories tonight, I truly do."

Although the dinner an inconvenience to Juliana, she still wanted to make an effort to be enthusiastic as she could for Gracie's sake. At least they'd not been dragged over and made to sit with the trustees. That was something to appreciate.

The doors opened and two white-gloved servants gestured toward the right. "Here for the banquet, ladies?"

"Yes, indeed we are!" Gracie's breathy voice made Juliana smile.

The young fellow on the right looked familiar. His wide eyes remained fixed on the beautiful girl standing before him.

"Frankie Quinlain?" It couldn't be.

"One and the same." He answered, but his eyes remained glued on Gracie. Finally, the gangly youth turned to her. "Oh, hello there."

Juliana arched an eyebrow at him. "You're all grown up, Frankie." In a flash, she felt so much older. Here was one of her best friend's brothers, a little devil when he was young, now standing here guarding the door.

He blinked rapidly. "I'll tick off your name, Juliana, that is Miss Beauchamps. You're still unmarried, aren't you?"

Heat flushed her cheeks. He knew full well how Aleksanteri had abandoned her weeks before their wedding. The whole parish knew.

"She won't be unwed for long, though." Gracie giggled. "A millionaire from Wisconsin is courting her."

Juliana began to gasp in protest, but her assistant elbowed her.

Behind them, someone laughed softly. She dare not turn to look.

Frankie waved them forward. "You're seated at Table Three."

A familiar voice demanded, "Young man, put me at Table Three as well."

A suit-jacketed arm flashed past her, a silver dollar extended and snatched up by Frankie. "Of course sir."

James Yost. She might as well just die now and sink into the wool carpeting, through the flooring, and beneath the building into the ground. He had to have heard Gracie's words.

"Oh, Mr. Yost!" The blonde pressed her hands to her pretty mouth as she swiveled around to face him.

Juliana cringed. It would be rude to ignore the man, wouldn't it? Ever so slowly, she turned and he immediately took her hand and raised it to his lips. Then he drew her arm through his and escorted her into the dining hall, Gracie trailing them.

She'd never been so mortified in all her life. All eyes were trained on them. *Thank you, Jesus, that the board isn't inside yet.* But what would they think once they saw she and Gracie seated with the wealthy man?

Carefully keeping her full skirt in hand, she maneuvered between the tables.

Mr. Yost indicated that Gracie should slide in next to Juliana. "Ladies, you are both looking radiant this evening." He assisted them each with their chairs.

"Thank you." Her assistant beamed up at him. "This is so exhilarating."

A warm smile made the beer baron's handsome face even more attractive. Oh, how could Gracie have told Frankie that a millionaire from Wisconsin was pursuing her? Surely Mr. Yost guessed her assistant was referring to him.

"How kind of you, Mr. Yost." Juliana had to watch her conversation with the man. If the board members watched her, they could get wrong notions.

She glanced around the room, enjoying the many floral arrangements. How odd that none had lilacs in them. Their perfume and spiky blossoms made them perfect in large bouquets this time of year.

At the far end of the room, seated in the center of the next to the last table, a dark-haired young man stared at her. Clean-shaven, she could see the deep cleft in his chin. Merely gazing at him took what breath she had away. Sister Mary Lou shouldn't have laced this corset so tight. Although it did exaggerate her curves. And why was she thinking such thoughts? That man was likely many years her junior. She averted her gaze. Why was the attractive stranger sitting all alone?

After he had settled into his shield-back cherrywood seat across from them, Mr. Yost leaned in. "I do hope you don't mind me presuming that I'd be welcome at your table." His features tugged in concern.

Was the man actually sensitive that he might be unwelcome? Juliana sat up more straight and forced a broad smile. "Why, sir, how could we not be pleased?"

"Of course you are, Mr. Yost." Gracie's sweet laugh had a calming effect on Juliana. "In fact, I was just speaking of you, sir."

Yes—saying Yost planned to marry her. The peaceful feeling screamed its way out of the room. Juliana discreetly slid her hand toward Gracie's and pinched her.

"Ouch!" She rubbed her hand and frowned at Juliana.

James Yost hiked an eyebrow. They were at a table not far from the entrance, so now they had the advantage of observing others as they entered. "My dear ladies, you look as though something is troubling you."

"No, I'm a little tired is all." She'd been surprised at how exhausted she'd felt since the fire and returning to work. And now she had an especially long day with this event and had to work on the morrow.

Gracie raised her crystal goblet of water to her lips and took a sip before lowering it slowly. "I think we all have a lot on our minds, Mr. Yost."

"Is that so?" Sitting this close, Juliana could see the silver threads in his hair. At least he was probably closer to her age than Richard Christy was. Not that it mattered, as neither man had made any profession of love. Oh, to have a charmer like Elizabeth Barrett Browning had in her husband.

"I don't know, Mr. Yost, unless you have a job for me." Was Gracie actually batting her long eyelashes at the man?

"A job?" His eyes widened, more like the look of a child caught with his hand in the cookie jar than a man actually surprised.

Juliana clenched her jaw. She'd failed to pursue a certain contract for her assistant once she turned eighteen. Even so, how could Gracie live on that pittance of a salary? The Beauchamp family did still have an empty cottage on their property. But she'd not discuss that in front of Mr. Yost. Why was Gracie being so bold? *Because she's desperate.* And Juliana had failed her.

Chapter 9

The wait staff led a trio of elderly matrons to their table, interrupting Juliana's thoughts. The women's gowns were spectacular, as were the diamonds glittering around their necks. They were seated further down their table, their husbands assisting them with the heavy chairs. Juliana didn't recognize any of them. Perhaps they were summer residents. But Mr. Yost raised his hand briefly to a silver-haired gentleman in a perfectly-tailored navy blue dinner jacket. The man nodded in return, his moustache twitching slightly. His wife glowered at Gracie and Juliana. *What in the world?*

"Excuse my distraction, ladies, that's an old friend of mine. He owns a competing brewery in Milwaukee." He gestured for the waiter to come to him. "Might you bring my wine now?"

The young man's hands trembled, at his sides. "No spirits until after the meal has been served. Sorry, Mr. Yost."

Their dinner mate waved him away, frowning, but the servant remained. "Shall I pour your tea, sir?"

"I don't suppose I could persuade you to substitute bourbon for my tea, can I?" Mr. Yost grumbled.

"No, sir. Mrs. Jeffries was adamant." The way the young man rubbed his fingers together, it appeared his hands itched for a bribe. If the rich man could slip him a coin, the servant couldn't accept—not with the inn owner standing guard over the room, just beyond them.

Yost made a disgusted snorting sound.

This was the first pique Juliana had ever viewed in James Yost. Did he have a drinking problem? He didn't act anything like her brother did, though.

Gracie surprised her, by reaching across the table and gently touching the man's burly hand. "Why should you need alcohol, when you've got the company of the prettiest and smartest woman in town?" She released his hand and pointed to Juliana.

"Gracie," she croaked. But then she decided to turn the tables on the person who made her want to slide under and hide beneath this very table. "I think you must mean yourself, not me."

The beer baron glanced between the two of them. "I should be counting my blessings at being in such splendid company—you are correct." He poured himself a glass of tea from the silver pitcher and then did so for them.

"Thank you." Gracie gazed intently at him. "When I don't get what I want I try to stay happy anyway. And I pray. Like I have prayed about a job. And a place to live."

A slow grin tipped Yost's lips. "I have no wine—but jobs I have aplenty. You were saying?"

"It's just that, well, I didn't want to say, but my birthday is coming up and…"

As the two began to chat about Gracie's predicament, Juliana watched their dinner partner's bright eyes. James Yost was quite possibly the most impressive and focused man she'd ever met. The few private conversations they'd had about library science and management of large facilities helped her realize how well-educated and intelligent he was. On the other hand, she still sensed an invisible hand holding her back. Maybe he did have a secret temper and alcohol problems.

Juliana still felt the young ebony-haired man's eyes on her, from the other end of the room. There was something very familiar about him. And a pleasing countenance that took her breath away. She allowed herself to look at him again, but the handsome man's eyes were focused on something behind her.

Gracie elbowed her and Juliana stifled a protest. "Look, there's Mr. Christy."

She daren't move. What was Richard doing here? Oh...the connection with Mrs. Jeffries, that had to be it. But instead of Richard, or his younger brother Garrett, as she turned she spied a much more mature-looking version of the youngest Christy. The man could have been Richard's brother, Garrett, but aged forward about twenty five years. He had to be the patriarch of the Christy family. On his arm, a lovely woman, in a gown even more old-fashioned than her own, entered with all the grace of a queen. Her features resembled Cordelia Jeffries'— perhaps her sister. Then Josephine and her fiancé Tom followed. And Garrett with Rebecca Hart. Where was Richard?

The three couples continued down the aisle between the tables and stopped where the handsome young man waited. He rose, bringing more, and more, and more of his tall frame into view. It couldn't be. No. But it was. It was Richard—all six feet six inches of him. Her mouth fell open. She closed it and swallowed.

Yost leaned in. "Are you all right? You look like you've seen a specter."

A waiter arrived and offered coffee, sparing Juliana from responding to his question.

Not only had his attempt to spiff up failed, but his efforts had failed miserably, judging from the look on Miss Beauchamps' pretty face. She looked even more aghast than she had at the library. Richard exhaled loudly and leaned back in his too-small chair. On the opposite side of the table sat Pa, with Cordelia Jeffries' sister, Irene St. Clair, beside him. Past her, Ox sat next to Rebecca.

Seated beside him, his sister pressed his hand. "What's wrong? Did my little brother get his heart broken already, with that magnificent face showing?"

Tom had the nerve to lean in across her and laugh at him. Richard scowled back.

"What's that?" Pa inclined his head. "Don't tell me another one of my children is lovesick. Not sure I could bear it."

Jo snapped open her napkin and arranged it on her lap. "I'm not lovesick, Pa."

Pa snorted. "Until you're proper married, I'm believin' you are, baby girl."

Resting on his elbows, Richard cast a red-faced Tom his own smart-alecky look. "Yup, yer right, Pa. Leastwise Tom is lovesick." He chuckled.

Ox snatched a roll from the basket and tossed it across the table at Richard. He caught it mid-air. His brother wrapped an arm around Rebecca. "Nah, Pa. Moose is fine and dandy."

If only they knew. He caught Juliana Beauchamps sneaking a peek in his direction and tried to hold her gaze, but she looked away. A pretty pink flush crept up her neck. *Maybe she does like me after all—and she will attend the ball with me.* But why was she seated by James Yost, the beer baron? What chance did he have against that man and his money? None.

Might as well face facts.

Just as the waiters, at the far end of the room, began to move forward, a solemn group of suited men streamed into the room together. None paused to exchange greetings with fellow diners, some of whom waved or nodded as the men passed. And at the front of them was Juliana's foe. Now if only Hatchens would sit near enough that Richard could overhear what they were discussing tonight.

Juliana's face drained of color and her mouth pulled in tightly. She grabbed her water glass and took a drink. If Richard was seated by her, instead of Yost, he'd reassure her. And why had he failed to invite her himself? Because he'd become a coward after seeing her at dinner with Yost. Something boiled up in him. *Never been a quitter before— ain't gonna start now.*

He had to fight for her.

"Iced tea, sir?" A waiter held out a silver pitcher. "Sorry, Mr. Christy, but I can't get any closer."

The trustees, being seated at the table behind them, made it impossible for the man to pour from the expected position, at each person's shoulder. Richard passed his crystal glass to the waiter.

Tom scowled. "The Library trustees sure relished their grand entrance."

Jo leaned in. "At least they're quiet."

The servant quickly filled the glasses and then stepped back between two of the tables as the trustees passed.

Pa's nostrils flared and his bushy eyebrows bunched. "Why, they have no better manners than a bunch of polecats settin' up waitin' on a trash can to overturn."

Mrs. St. Clair raised her napkin to her mouth and appeared to be covering a laugh. "Well, they've managed to get everyone's attention, haven't they?"

Tom exhaled loudly. "If that's what they've wanted then they've achieved it."

Cordelia, dressed in a lace-covered gown, moved to the banquet hall's center. "Now that we have all arrived and been seated." She cast a look at the trustee's table, a tight smile on her face. "I'd like to welcome you to the grand opening of the inn, and in particular, welcome you to this hall, which we hope will serve the community for many years to come."

People began to applaud, so Richard did, too.

"We'll have some short speeches, but meanwhile my waiters will be coming through to serve your meal. You'll notice on your menu cards that we're serving Beef Bourguignon, whipped chived potatoes, assorted breads with fresh butter, and steamed asparagus for our main courses. For our grand finale, we offer chocolate mousse or apple torte served with whipped cream accompanied by café au lait, Café Americane, or hot tea."

The applause was more enthusiastic. The waiters pushed carts down the aisle, beginning at the farthest table.

"Well, of course they'd serve us first. We're the pillars of the community after all." Mr. Hatchens' nasally tone identified him immediately, and he was seated to Richard's left immediately behind him.

One of the men at the table snorted, while the rest made softer sounds of agreement.

Pa frowned. "Ya know they changed the serving from front to back, and switched it around just for the Christy family?" His loud voice was surely meant to carry to the trustees' ears.

"And the Jeffries," Tom chimed in. "Although, in particular for the Christy men because we dare not keep Richard or Garrett waiting too long on their food or there might be an uprising."

Jo elbowed Tom. "Behave."

"What? It's the truth." Her fiancé leaned in to kiss her.

"We're in public, son." But Pa's voice was light-hearted. He'd called Tom *son*. Would Rebecca be called daughter? And what about Juliana?

Behind them, Hatchens' barked out, "And before our windbag of a mayor gets up there, let me announce that we will be working on staffing issues tonight."

"Oh?" One of his cronies asked.

"Indeed. I've seen vexing issues with the female staff at our venerable institution. I want to propose some immediate solutions."

Richard strained to listen, but he heard no comments pro or con over the soft discussions going on at his own table. Pa narrowed his eyes and Richard made the gesture for don't ask, and his father winked at him. He looked past Richard, scanned the table behind him filled with the trustees, then ducked his chin as though indicating he'd watch, too.

The mayor, a kind man who supported both the library and the orphanage, spoke about the town being on the cusp of bigger things and how the history of the area had always been inclusive. Apparently not inclusive enough so to keep his library board members from wanting women out. But maybe the mayor didn't know that.

After the mayor had finished, Reverend Jones, the pastor from their church, and Father Paul, from the Roman Catholic Church, each spoke and said prayers. Both were good speakers and didn't throw in a bunch of fancy words that just confused people.

Reaching behind Jo's back, Tom tapped Richard and whispered, "Reverend Jones is doing a good job of counseling us. According to Ox..." he jerked a thumb in Garrett's direction "you're supposed to be getting some sessions in with the pastor, too!" Tom laughed.

Richard scowled at his sister, hoping for an explanation. She shrugged. He nudged her toe under the table. She moved her feet away. He positioned his chair so close to hers that she was sandwiched between him and Tom. She crossed her arms.

"What is your fiancé talking about?" Richard whispered in her ear.

Jo gestured for him to scoot away from her and he did. Just a little, then he cocked an eyebrow at her, waiting. Finally, she sighed and pointed to Ox, whose sleepy eyes suggested he wasn't paying any attention to the pastor's words. "Garrett got it in his head that you and Juliana have plans and are merely waiting to set the date."

"What plans?"

"For marriage you log-headed man."

He jerked backward in his seat, afraid for a moment that he might tip over. "Where would he get such a notion?"

Pa, who'd still faced him, but appeared to be giving Reverend Jones' words consideration, finally held a finger to his mouth to shush them. Richard exhaled loudly. He'd have to straighten Ox out later. Given everything he'd heard at church stump meetings, the responsibility a man had to his wife was immense. God sure asked a lot from a fella. Seemed like the wife got a better deal, even if she didn't reckon so. If a husband abided by what the Good Book said, then the wife was getting a plum good specimen of a man. Pa had been like that with Ma. But could Richard be that kind of husband himself? No sense worryin' since there were no prospects now—not with James Yost fawning over Juliana. Heck, the camp wasn't even set up. He shouldn't even be thinkin' on such things. He swallowed hard and glanced at Juliana and Yost. He couldn't just leave her to that man's devices, could he?

After the preachers had finished talking, conversations resumed. Since Richard didn't have a dinner companion, it wasn't hard for him to simply eat, enjoy and hopefully eavesdrop on the library board.

"Delicious," Pa pronounced.

Richard took a forkful of the beef. "Easier to eat without a beard, too."

Ox ran a hand along his jaw. "Reckon it's easier to kiss Juliana, too, ain't it?"

So much for a private conversation. "Miss Beauchamps is a fine young lady and ya shouldn't..." he searched for the fancy words Tom had taught him, "ya shouldn't cast aspersions on her character."

A muscle in Ox's cheek jerked and Rebecca whispered in his ear before addressing Richard. "It is not vulgar for engaged couples to engage in a kiss."

Richard shook his head. "I reckon that's true. But seein' as me and Miss Beauchamps aren't courtin', much less getting married, that wouldn't apply, would it?"

Rebecca and Ox exchanged a confused glance. Where on earth had they gotten their ill-conceived notion? At the other end of the room, sat Miss Juliana Beauchamps, with whom he supposedly needed to "set a date" and apparently she was mighty cozy with James Yost. So instead of worrying himself, he focused on digging into his food.

Once in a while his sister or brother would ask him something to which he'd nod and smile. That discouraged them from working too hard at getting him to do much talking. But he heard Hatchens loud and clear—there was only one windbag in the room and it wasn't the mayor. Richard didn't need to stay after the banquet was over to know what was going to be proposed. Every other comment the man made was a complaint about Juliana and her assistant. At one point, he heard one of the men turn in his chair, to look at her.

"Why that is her with James Yost, isn't it. Mr. Hatchens, you have no worries as far as dismissing her. From the looks of things, perhaps our new friend will whisk her off to Wisconsin."

"He's a married man," one of the men hissed.

The hairs on the back of Richard's neck rose. He watched as James Yost slid his hand across to Juliana's hand and gave it a squeeze. Of all the low life, low down, men… He ought to go introduce Yost to his friends, Mr. Fists.

"You're misinformed," Hatchens growled. "His wife died last winter from pneumonia."

A widower then. Richard's ire diminished and he suddenly felt sorry for the man. There'd been no mention of his marital status in the papers, but the social section implied he was single and highly sought after. Rich or not, to lose one's wife had to be awful. But at least he'd known the joy of marriage. Across the table, Pa's face looked peaceful for the first time in a very long time. Mrs. St. Clair seemed to be the right match for him despite their differences. And finally, Pa had come out of the dark place he'd isolated himself in after Ma's death.

"Doesn't change the fact that our head librarian is cavorting around town with him," another board member groused.

"They didn't arrive together," Hatchens stated. "Mr. Yost and I were supposed to walk over together. I'd invited him to sit at our table."

Richard took a bite of his potatoes, the savory puff melting in his mouth.

He strained to hear another man's soft voice, "I figured with his experience funding the building of the new library in Milwaukee, that Mr. Yost would have good insight for us."

Which was what type of insight? By the time Hatchens spoke again, Richard had finished cutting his asparagus into tiny pieces.

"Mr. Yost has an offer for us that may solve some of our dilemmas."

Was that how the officious man thought of Juliana? As a dilemma? And who was their other one?

He'd find a way to help Juliana. He had to. His heart wouldn't allow otherwise.

Chapter 10

"Here's another directive from the board." Hatchens slid a missive across the shiny surface of her worktop. He wore a jolly expression, as though he was Pére Noel delivering her Christmas present.

Behind him, Gracie rolled her eyes as she carried an armful of books to the children's circle.

Juliana forced her features into what she hoped was a courteous, submissive expression, all the while battling the urge to take the letter, tear it into tiny little pieces, and dump them over the horrid man's head. But she needed this job. "I'll read it right after I've completed the children's program."

Her obsequious expression must have worked, because he didn't challenge her statement. As he departed the library, she exhaled a long, slow puff of air and sank back onto her wooden stool.

Gracie hurried toward her, one of Claudette's old Sunday dresses swirling around her legs. She leaned in across the counter. "Have you seen Mr. Christy? The children are asking for his Bon Jean stories."

"I'll be there in a minute." She eyed the envelope.

She'd cut back on wearing her bicycling outfits to work, particularly the bloomers, after the long and scathing memo she'd received from the Library Board. So, now, unless the day was mild like today, Juliana would have to take her mother's carriage and pay for the boarding and livery in town since they'd limited her transportation. But she'd walked the miles to work this morning, thinking about Mr. Hatchens with each step. Would the train be stopping at the Christy Lumber

Camp? But the locomotive that would go should be a different kind of train, with a flat bed, mainly for hauling freight and logs. And she couldn't picture herself hopping on the back of it like the lumberjacks might. She exhaled a long sigh. Maybe she could ask her friend, Janet, if Labrons Store was doing deliveries to the camp, or she'd add that of her list of things to ask Richard.

Bon Jean never showed up that day. Juliana wished she could fuss just as the children had when he failed to arrive. One of the town children, listening to the story on the edge of the circle, had piped up and shared that Richard made the Bible come to life. Wouldn't that be nice, if like Papa, Richard read the Bible to her after dinner?

As the day came to a close, Juliana fingered the latest dictate from the board. *Any volunteers at the library shall first be approved by the board. All must submit to an interview.* What satisfaction she would have later that night, in burning the new mandate in the cookstove fire. She crumpled the paper and shoved it in her pocket. So now they were taking away her Bon Jean.

"What a long and disappointing day." Juliana sighed and brushed her hair from her forehead as she and Gracie left the library building and locked up.

Outside the back door, Richard paced. He glanced up at them. Although he appeared much younger without his beard, if possible, he was even better looking. "You're walking today, Miss Beauchamps?"

She gestured to the empty bike stand. "As you can see."

"Why's that?" He rubbed his jaw.

"I recently received a memo from the board. Apparently, riding a bicycle isn't considered ladylike." And another edict had been issued that day, which would likely keep Bon Jean from entertaining the children again. At least at the library. Maybe they could work something else out. But what, she didn't know. Perhaps something at the orphanage, after work. Soon Richard would be busy with the demands of his camp and likely unavailable to volunteer.

Gracie snorted. "No one else has ever complained about her biking. In fact, many of the women in town ride regularly. And there's a new bicycling club forming—not that I own a bike, but for those who do, such as Miss Beauchamps."

"As it is, I'll have to shun my bicycle and walk, for now." As often as she could, anyway.

A breeze ruffled the leaves on the nearby oak tree and tousled Richard's hair. "But you do have a pair of fine mares, if I recollect properly."

She exhaled loudly. "We do, but with two families now sharing them, I can't drive the carriage in, so I'm walking." And four more mouths to feed, plus the orphans who continued to visit. Not that she resented them, but her faith in God's provision was being stretched so thin, it may snap.

"Come on with me, I'll give you a ride." He grinned down at her and she averted her eyes as heat singed her cheeks.

Why hadn't he come by the library that day? She'd watched the clock, hoping and praying, but he'd disappointed her—and now here he was. "What are you doing in town?" Her voice emerged as a whine and she gritted her teeth. She sounded like she owned him. And here he'd just offered her a ride. She should be happy, grateful even.

"I 'spect I can come to town just like any fella." Richard's words held a tease.

"But you didn't come into the library." And now it sounded like she was accusing him of a felony. It wasn't Juliana's business if he chose to not come by. Had a board member said something to him?

Gracie giggled. "Was it because I had to fuss at those shanty boys of yours for falling asleep in the back stacks a few days ago?"

"No." He frowned. "I interviewed some cook candidates for the camp."

Juliana's sister-in-law had mentioned she'd seen the Christy Lumber Camp ad, in the newspaper they subscribed to at home. With all of the children battling the flux, Melanie was loathe to leave them to come interview. And how would she be able to work with three young children at home, anyway? "Any success?"

"None."

"Sorry."

He twisted his cap in his hands. "Don't know what I'll do, Juliana. If I don't get some awful good cooks, I'll be outta business right quick."

"I've got an idea, but I'm not sure." Her family's property was not more than two to three miles from Christy camp. Even if the children were sick, couldn't one of the women stay home to watch while the other two went to cook? And could Mother and Claudette help a little until he secured full time cooks?

He walked so closely beside her, on the walkway, that his wool plaid jacket brushed against her arms. She looked up, up into his dark eyes and warmth spread through her chest. How could she tell this man that he had to submit to an interrogation by the board before he returned to her story circle? If he could manage to get past Mr. Hatchens, which was doubtful.

They paused and Richard turned toward her and took her hand. He leaned in. Was he…going to kiss her? Right there on the city's main thoroughfare?

"Miss Beauchamps, there is something I have to tell you. It's been on my mind and my heart for a little while now."

Oh heavens, was he going to share his feelings right there in front of Gracie? She pressed a hand to her heart.

Gracie giggled. "I better scoot on back to the orphanage and see how Sister Mary Lou is feeling. Have a good evening, you two."

Gazing down at her, love shone in Richard's eyes. Or was it concern? Or respect for an older female friend? "I should have said something earlier."

Juliana pulled her hand free and held it up, to stop him. He may be handsome and sweet, and wonderful with the children, but wasn't Juliana too many years his senior? With his beard shaved off and Jo Christy's pronouncement that Richard was her "baby brother", could anything further ever come of their friendship? "Mr. Christy, you are much too young…"

"No, Juliana, I'm not too young." He met her gaze and held it.

Her heart leapt in her chest. Did he know her age?

He cleared his throat. "You see, I understand men like Hatchens—they're always trying to work a situation out for themselves."

"Hatchens?" She frowned.

"I'm old enough to know a scoundrel when I see one."

"What?" She clamped her lips shut. What was he talking about? Had he heard about the latest mandate? This was making no sense.

"I reckon I shoulda said somethin' earlier. But now I'm not sure what's to be done."

She found her voice. "About?"

Richard ran his tongue over his lower lip. "Ya see, Hatchens has got kin he wants to put to work at the library—to take your place."

Her mouth went dry. "What?" She was beginning to sound like a parrot. Juliana's heartbeat quickened. She couldn't lose her job. What would she do?

"His nephew's gonna be done with college any day and Hatchens has offered him a job up here. Hatchens is tryin' to get the board to approve him."

"But I have a contract." Which ended in thirty days and would need to be renewed and hadn't yet. Her stomach spasmed.

"That might be, but…" He turned her toward the street and pointed to his buggy. "Let me get you home and I'll tell you all I've learned so far."

"So you're my spy?" Did she really like the sounds of this? No—but it was a relief to know someone had her back covered. Like her brothers used to do for her.

He laughed. "I reckon so."

When they reached the open carriage he swooped her up by the waist and placed her on the passenger side. "Oh!" When he released her, she missed the warmth of his hands, and his strength.

"Sorry, didn't mean to scare ya."

Soon they were on their way and he explained what had happened so far. She shook her head, a pall of shock dampening her senses.

"Listen to me, Juliana. Don't change a thing yer doin'. That man has it in for you, and I don't know why the good Lord is allowin' this but one thing is for sure and for certain—the Lord is in control."

"If you believe that, then why are you skulking around?"

He scratched his head. "Wasn't skulkin', was tryin' to get at the truth."

If she lost her job... "I support my mother and my sister—and as you know, they both have physical ailments and are unable to work." Juliana chewed on her lower lip and stared down at her hands.

"Yes'm, I know that, but they seem to be improvin'." He grinned at her in approval. "I like a woman with pluck, and you got that in spades."

She shook her head but couldn't help laughing. "Pluck, but possibly no job soon."

"We'll keep prayin' about that—and about finding me some cooks." A muscle twitched in his cheek. "I sure couldn't picture a pretty little gal like you out there cookin' for a bunch of shanty boys."

Juliana blinked in confusion. "Thank you for the compliment. But you're wrong." He must not know that once she and Aleksanteri were wed she was to have cooked for his parents' camp. But after he'd left, Papa sent her off to school in lower Michigan. And she'd become a librarian.

"I ain't wrong about you being beautiful. I've got two good eyes in my head." He pointed to the dark orbs.

"Well, thank you. But you're wrong about my capabilities, or lack thereof."

He flicked the reins and the horse pulled the carriage from the curb. As they departed town, church members waved at them, and men lifted their hats. It seemed half the city was out, now that the weather was improving and the tourists hadn't yet descended upon them. Soon they were outside of town and beneath the canopy of fir, pine, oak, and maple. The spinster librarian with the handsome Paul Bon Jean, or rather, Richard Christy.

Next to her on the bench seat, his presence loomed larger than life. How many times had she imagined the real Bon Jean arriving here? And he always brought, with him, her older brothers who'd been lost in the war; the Beauchamps brothers she'd never had the chance to grow up and know. In reality, her brothers' remains were buried far from home, all alone. In her imaginings, however, Gerard, Emmett, and Pierre hadn't really died in the Civil War. In her childhood fantasies, the heroic Paul Bon Jean had stomped down to the battle fields in Virginia, rescued her brothers, and brought them to his mystical lumber camp in Canada. There the three brothers worked as lumberjacks, chopping down the mighty trees across Canada. One day she would have met those hardworking brothers. She wiped away a tear.

"You okay?" He transferred the reins to one hand and wrapped the other around her and pulled her close. She didn't resist, but leaned in against his broad shoulder. "Don't ya worry none. It will be all right."

She wanted to believe him. As they rode through the woods, the fresh scent of pines and new growth on the hardwoods permeated the air. She breathed in deeply. Her family had been here generations, and God had always seen them through.

"Right pretty back here, ain't it? I've enjoyed my rides out to the new camp." But he looked down into her eyes with something she could only construe as adoration. Then he focused on the road, again.

They exited into the clearing and onto the sandy road that led to their little compound.

He whistled as they approached the half-circle drive. "That view of the lake never stops giving me chills of appreciation. It's so darned beautiful."

She shrugged and removed his arm from her shoulder. Didn't need Mother and Claudette seeing them and getting the wrong idea. "Guess I'm used to it."

"How do you get used to something so lovely, that's always changin'?" The warmth in his voice suggested he was talking about something else entirely and sent a shiver through her.

He assisted her down from the buggy, holding her aloft for a moment, eye-to-eye, her feet dangling over the ground. "Juliana, we're gonna beat old Hatchens at his own game, you wait and see."

His face was so close to hers, his almost black eyes much lighter this close, with flecks of amber in them and a dark gray rim. His lips were full and pink and right there where she was looking. He cleared his throat and chuckled then lowered her to the ground. Her legs wobbled and he took her arm.

Later, after he'd stayed for dinner, at Mother's insistence, all the Beauchamps women fussed over him, Melanie in particular.

"Are you sure you didn't coax me out here just to get me to hire your sister-in-law?" Richard accepted a third helping of biscuits and gravy.

Where did that man put all the food he ate?

Melanie leaned in on her elbows, hanging on his every word when he sampled each dish.

But it was Claudette who surprised her most. She set the apple cobbler in front of Richard, as though prepared for him alone, and beside that, she'd added one of Mother's best china bowls full of whipped cream, which had to have taken her over a half hour to prepare, even with using the rotary beater. Her younger sister stood over the tall man now, her slim arm draped across the back of his chair for all the world as though taking possession of him.

Juliana didn't like it. Not one bit. She tried to catch her younger sister's attention but failed.

"Please, Mr. Christy. You try it first. You'll see I'm a good cook and I'd love to be hired full time at the camp—for once all the men get here, too."

Full time? Juliana's jaw dropped. Their mother didn't so much as raise an eyebrow at this comment.

"Reckon ya have fed the handful of us well out there." Richard looked across the dish-strewn table at her, his lips twitching.

Juliana tried to consider how Richard might see her sister. Golden, wavy hair trailed to a slender waist. Her too-small dress hugged decidedly feminine curves. Goodness, Claudette needed new clothing and soon. Perfect beautiful features set in ivory skin, with her large blue-green eyes focused only on him. Juliana's heartbeat struggled into a faster erratic beat in protest. She patted her mouth, her too-small mouth compared to her sister's, and set her napkin on her lap.

Claudette was also closer in age to Richard.

Juliana pushed back her chair from the table, the wooden legs scraping against the floor. "I'll clean up."

"We'll help." Her sister-in-law left the table.

Mother shook her head. "No, Melanie, you go take care of the children. And Juliana you take a rest—go down by the beach and sit a spell. I want to talk with Mr. Christy."

Carrying plates to the sink, she overheard Claudette's soft voice. "Should I stay, Mother?"

"Yes, my dear. Sit down."

Juliana and Melanie left the house.

"Do you think he'll hire all three of us?" Melanie wrung her hands. "I pray so."

"What?" Had Melanie lost her mind?

Later, after a long walk during which she'd swatted away more mosquitoes and black flies than she cared to count, Juliana returned with a sprig of lilac in her hand, as Richard was exiting the house.

He gave her a lopsided grin. "Seems I've hired me three new cooks."

"My sister isn't able…" She waved the lilac springs before her.

He raised a large hand and backed away. "Let's see what she can do, all right?"

Then he headed out, as though they'd both just experienced another fire, as he sprinted to his carriage.

As she lamented his departure, Juliana inhaled the lilac. Too bad the growing season was so short. There was so little time to enjoy them—and then they were gone.

Richard had dodged a bullet, or rather a sneezing spell, before he'd left Juliana. A shame to have to depart so quickly, but he daren't risk an attack in front of her. No self-respecting man would. What would she think of him if he had?

Now, after enjoying the Beauchamps ladies' company and good cooking, Richard's drive out to the camp seemed lonely. Too much so. The handful of men in the camp could take care of themselves. Probably knee-deep into a game of pinochle, already. He needed to talk with Tom—see what he'd heard about the board members. Richard directed the horses to the fork in the road and headed toward town. A handful of men, inhabiting what would become a bustling lumber camp, just wasn't normal. Good thing Mrs. Jeffries had said that he was always welcome.

Did I do right, Lord? Offering to hire all three women? Sure, Juliana's little sister couldn't keep up with those other ladies, but if she could peel taters and carrots and help out even half a day--that was something, wasn't it? He wasn't about to tell Juliana of his concerns, lest she think he was giving charity. Come to think of it, he'd probably not tell Pa until they'd all gotten settled in. He had to believe that God had provided for his imminent need. Even if two of those three ladies could help, at least he wasn't empty-handed.

After he'd arrived and stabled the horse, Richard headed in, through the back of the inn. Dark had begun to settle in the skies, turning the heavens a deep blue. Instinctively, he locked the door behind him—he'd seen no light in his brother's work shed, so Ox was likely upstairs reading. Richard stepped into the kitchen. Empty.

He strode up the long hall. *No lights on in the family's dining room.* Maybe Tom was reading in the parlor. He headed down the hall. Hearing James Yost's distinctive voice, Richard stopped short. Up till now, he'd been able to avoid the man when he was at the inn. For some reason, Yost had chosen to stay at Cordelia's Inn when he'd returned from Milwaukee. Edging up to the parlor's entryway, Richard spied Hatchens' profile as he lifted a teacup from its dainty saucer. *What kind of man sips tea—and from a cup that small, anyway?* Richard ducked back behind the wall. What were they doing there? True, Yost was welcome to visit with anyone he chose, but why Hatchens? Richard leaned against the cool plastered wall.

"We're so happy to have you staying with us on this visit." Cordelia's voice carried into the darkened hallway where only a couple of gaslights flickered on low.

"It's been delightful, but I need to return to work and get back home, again."

"Your assistant said you're greatly needed in Milwaukee. You have some needs at the factory, I believe." Leave it to Cordelia to get that information out of Yost's sidekick.

"Indeed, I do. And Milwaukee is a lovely place. Not so charming as here. But, yes, I need to return promptly."

Richard stifled the urge to sneeze. Someone must have brought more of those blasted lilacs into the building. Sure enough, right down the hall, on a half-circular cherry table, beneath one of the gaslamps, a large bouquet featured spikes of the purple flower. He tried holding his breath.

"And so you've determined you need help with your personal library, is that correct?" Hatchens' actually sounded happy for once.

"Yes, the public library is beginning to settle in. We still have some positions to fill but we're confident we shall place some of the top candidates soon."

"Very admirable." Father Paul's words startled Richard. What was the priest doing there?

Richard exhaled slowly and tried breathing through his mouth.

"Indeed, and I would be most grateful to both of you men if your very capable librarian and her lovely assistant could accompany me back to help me in my personal endeavors."

Juliana and Gracie? Richard pinched his nose. He couldn't sneeze just now. Had to listen.

"Personal endeavors?" The priest's skeptical tone contrasted with the earlier warm response.

"That is, since the private library is in my home..."

So he'd take the young women to his own place? Richard pinched his nose tighter, drawing in slow breaths through his mouth.

"A mansion from what I've seen—simply beautiful." Mr. Hatchens intoned. "I'm sure they'd be very comfortable."

Richard would give Hatchens the comfort of his own bed, too, after he'd gotten a whoopin'. What was the ignorant man thinking? Richard had to calm his anger. Surely God wouldn't let two innocent women go off with this man. Maybe the newspapers didn't print the truth about him.

"Thank you." Yost's self-satisfied voice grated on Richard's nerves. "As I was telling Father Paul, since the library is in my home, it makes this a personal task."

"I see. But Gracie is too young to serve as chaperone to Miss Beauchamps." Father Paul didn't sound convinced of this idiotic plan, either.

"She'd suggested that Sister Mary Lou could use a rest. I could ensure that your orphanage supervisor could be well tended to, trust me. She'd serve solely in a spiritual capacity to the young ladies, and not work on the library whatsoever."

"So she'd chaperone?" The priest still sounded doubtful.

"Sister Mary Lou does need a good break—she's been looking rather piqued lately." Cordelia's words steamed Richard up. How could she encourage this folly?

"And we, at the Board of Trustees for the Library, could certainly make an exception for Miss Beauchamps and her assistant to be gone for say—four weeks?" Hatchens spoke in his confident and supercilious manner as though all was a done deal.

"A month would be fine." Yost almost gloated. The man already counted his victory.

A month? She'd be at this man's home a full month? Richard focused his attention on not sneezing but was becoming light-headed.

"Of course, I could get my nephew to help out at the library, for that time, and we have our summer library interns."

Juliana had said nothing about helping Yost with his library. Did she even know anything about this? As likely as hens having teeth.

"Is your nephew done with his schooling?" Cordelia, his betrayer, acted as though this plan was just fine.

"Yes, recently graduated—summa cum laude."

"Impressive." Yost's single word held a heavy German accent that sometimes appeared in his speech.

"I thought so." *That simpering pole cat Hatchens would think so.*

"So, do we have a solution to my problem?"

"Let me see." Father Paul intoned. "I agree that our favorite nun needs a break. And I'd ask one thing of you, in return."

"Anything."

"Help Gracie find a suitable position in Milwaukee— perhaps as a nanny with a good family. Or in the new Milwaukee library that you helped build."

"Is she unhappy here?" Something about Yost's tone of voice sounded like he knew something he wasn't saying.

"She's about to age out of our orphanage, Mr. Yost. And I fear this area holds too many sad memories for the child. Gracie may benefit from a move."

Poor Gracie. Richard had no idea.

Hatchens cleared his throat. "She's very attached to Miss Beauchamps. Perhaps you may seek a permanent position there for the two of them? We'd hate to see them go, but we should consider her happiness, too. After all she's a spinster of twenty-eight, with no prospects here."

Twenty-eight? The first time he'd spied her she looked to be a child. But he'd immediately become aware she was a woman, albeit a tiny one, or petite, as Jo would put it. Why, thank God, she'd not been snapped up before now. And she did have prospects here—him being the primary one. Just as soon as he had something to offer her. But Yost—he had more. Richard's hopes yelled out "Timber!" as they crashed.

Hatchens cleared his throat. "I hate to state it so plainly, but I'm not a heartless man. My dear wife will attest that my heart holds only the greatest care for womankind. But I believe that lumberjack friend of hers lacks compassion for a woman's sensibilities."

"Oh?" Richard could picture Yost's ears' perking up.

"Yes. I overheard Christy announce that he has no intentions of marrying Miss Beauchamps. That said despite his constant hovering over her at the library."

Richard's loud sneeze reverberated in the hallway and he trotted his hasty retreat out the back.

Chapter 11

"Miss Beauchamps, may I have a word?" James Yost swooped in on Juliana, in the men's fiction section, where she was placing books in their proper Dewey decimal order.

"Of course."

"Fine job, by the way, of fully implementing Mr. Dewey's system." He offered his crooked, and charming, grin.

"It's how I was trained."

"One of the advantages of being a younger librarian from a progressive college." He briefly quirked his eyebrows, but his tone was serious.

The head librarian, whom she had replaced, had balked at the notion of bringing the library's holdings all in under this system and had ultimately resigned. "This is what the board wanted."

"I've actually come to beg your indulgence in a plan that has been approved, just now, by your board of trustees." He raised his arms and set his hands on either side of the bookcases, boxing her in.

"Oh?" She fought the urge to duck under his arms and bolt from the library. Dread coursed through her like being swallowed up in a huge Lake Michigan wave.

Mr. Yost beamed like a child with a new toy. "I've received permission for your friend, Miss, er, rather Sister Mary Lou, to accompany you and Miss Gracie to Milwaukee."

"Milwaukee?" She dipped her chin and rolled her eyes up at him as she often did with difficult patrons.

"You and Miss Gracie shall assist me in bringing order to my personal library." He tapped his fingers on the shelves.

Her heart hammered with such vigor she could hear it pumping in her ears. "In your home?"

"Yes. You'd each have your own suite. And a maid." He dropped his hands to his side. "We'd travel by steamship."

No contract had arrived yet for her nor for Gracie. She ran her tongue over her top lip and straightened. "Miss Gracie's compensation?"

He casually named an amount that equaled half of Juliana's yearly wages and she tried not to gasp. "And I shall make every effort to obtain suitable employment for her so she can remain in Milwaukee when you and Sister Mary Lou depart in a month."

"A month?" she croaked.

The wealthy man leaned in and raised his hand to his mouth as though to keep his words secret. "I have every hope that Sister Mary Lou will get the rest she so richly deserves, and shall return renewed with vigor."

Her friend refreshed, her assistant employed and resituated. How tempting. But what about Richard?

But with him being maybe twenty-three and she twenty-eight, how could this relationship work? No, it was not to be. He'd find a young bride who could bear him many little lumberjacks.

"I have a contract, though, Mr. Yost—that I am waiting on."

"You'll receive twice the amount Gracie is paid, plus I'm assured your contract will be waiting."

Her brain seemed to have stopped working when Mr. Yost said she'd receive twice Gracie's wages. Why, that was an entire year's worth of wages in one month! She could put money in the bank for Mother and Claudette and Melanie and the children. She refocused on Mr. Yost's words. Had he said, "when you return" or had he said, "*If* you return" just now? Had she imagined the latter?

Gracie would not be able to refuse this offer. And Juliana didn't see how she could, either. This must be the reason Mr. Hatchens was so happy. And perhaps he'd only hired his nephew to come because he'd had an inkling of Mr. Yost's plan. "Your offer is extremely generous, but…" What were his expectations?

"Let me assure you, all will be above board, Miss Beauchamps. I have a pristine reputation in the community to maintain."

But would she be back for The Lumberjacks' Ball? Did it matter? Perhaps some time apart would be good for her and Richard.

His eyes crinkled in compassion and he took her hand in his, his touch surprisingly gentle—like that of a father with a child. "I'm so distressed that Mr. Christy has no intention of courting you. He certainly gave every appearance of wishing to do so."

Heat rushed to her cheeks. So someone had pointed out their age difference. And Richard had made it clear he'd not be pursuing her. This revelation cemented her decision. Why bother worrying about the ball? "Sounds perfect, Mr. Yost."

The next day, after Juliana had explained everything to Claudette, both she and Melanie berated her for believing James Yost.

"Why do you think that rich man is telling you such an obvious story, Juliana?" Her sister-in-law poured herself another cup of coffee. "Don't be so naïve."

Claudette arched a golden brow. "Even I know these wealthy men think they can do as they please. Your reputation will be in tatters."

"But Sister Mary Lou will be with us." Juliana had already packed her clothes into Mother's leather-covered trunk.

"Richard Christy is in love with you, Juliana." Melanie sipped her coffee, made a face, and then reached for the sugar bowl.

Claudette wagged a finger at Juliana. "He's sweet on you. Don't give up on him!"

"Come out to the camp with us this morning. You'll have the rest of the afternoon to finish packing, if you don't believe us." Melanie poured more cream into her coffee and stirred, a dreamy look on her pretty face. "The look on his face, when he's with you, is just like your brother looked at me."

Juliana clasped Melanie's free hand. "I'm so sorry you lost him. I really am."

"Pascal died too young." Her sister-in-law wiped a tear from her cheek. "But that wasn't my point. It's that I'm concerned about this beer baron, and you need to be careful."

"And we need to test out our theory about where Richard's heart lies." Claudette pointed out the window to where Timmy, Marcus, and Stephen were loading small, immature lilac bushes into the back of their wagon.

Juliana stood to look out. Then she laughed.

Melanie set her coffee cup into her saucer with a loud clink. "Mr. Yost may be jealous of Richard and want to eliminate him as an option for your affections."

"Let's give Richard a chance to know where you stand with him. Make a lilac declaration of your intentions, Juliana." Claudette beamed.

Before she knew it, Juliana had been hustled off to the Christy Lumber Camp. Now, dressed in her clean work clothes, her hair upswept, and the back of the wagon full of immature lilac bushes, she was to try to elicit his attention.

This would be her test of Richard Christy's feelings for her. When she arrived, Juliana gathered the young lilac bushes from the back of the wagon and placed them into a child's wagon she'd borrowed from her sister-in-law. One by one, she set the trees and bushes into the bottom and then pulled it toward the main cabin in the camp. If Richard didn't get the hint by her planting the lilacs, then he never would. Those lilacs, and her bringing them here, were her bold pronouncement of her interest in him and of being with him. And he couldn't be so dense that he wouldn't understand that bringing her favorite flower to the camp meant she wanted to be there—near him. With him, if God so chose.

"Good afternoon, Miss Juliana." Sven pronounced her name like Huliana, which would have made her smile, had she not been so nervous.

"Good day."

"*Ja.* It is." Richard's assistant cocked his head at her. "Can we help you?"

"Maybe." Maybe not. "I'd like to spruce up around Richard's cottage—make it more homey."

"Ja. A good idea."

The camp handyman strode up. "What have we got here?"

"Lilacs for the lumber camp."

"Ja, and plenty of them, Mr. Bell," Sven informed the handyman.

A furrow formed between the man's eyebrows, and he didn't move, as though reluctant to comply. He looked familiar.

"Are you Avery Bell? My brothers' friend?" Mother had pointed him out long ago. Would her brothers, had they lived, appear much like this man, with lines etching their face and their hair streaked with gray? Or more like Richard's father, who appeared more vigorous and youthful? The Christy patriarch might even be younger than her eldest brother would have been. She swallowed.

"Yes, I am. And you must be Juliana—your Ma's comfort after she lost them. Sure do wish they'd come back home with me..."

"Me, too." Her childhood fantasy of her brothers being carried off by Paul Bon Jean took a beating.

"Avery." Sven's pronunciation drew the man's name out into three long syllables, like a parent did when trying to urge a child to do something. "Let me get a few shanty boys to help with those bushes."

"You going to have the men dig the spots for her plants, then, eh?"

"Ja," Sven called over his broad shoulder.

Avery shook his head first, but then smiled at her. "That man would have to be blind to ignore what you're offering him, Miss Beauchamps. And although I'm not a gambling man, I'm willing to bet not only will those lilacs be settled before sundown, but there's one exceptionally tall lumber camp boss who'll bend down on one knee." He winked at her and headed off toward one of the small buildings that encircled the yard.

Juliana patted her cheeks, still feeling the warmth from Mr. Bell's comment. Was he right? She hoped so. As she trod across the yard, she inhaled the invigorating scent of fresh lumber.

To her left a long, narrow building paralleled an older building—likely the single men's bunkhouse. Scattered around the land were small shack-like cottages. Those must be for the married men. But how did they get their wives to put up with such small quarters? She cringed. Maybe some of the lilacs should be planted around those tiny houses—to cheer up the occupants who'd soon arrive. Maybe if they knew their surroundings would be prettier in the spring…

The scent of smoked ham and something sweet, maybe cherry tarts, carried on the lake breeze. Juliana followed her nose to a large, rough wood building. Outside in the sunshine, seated on a bench, Claudette peeled potatoes. Standing over her, his back to Juliana, Richard talked with her. Juliana stilled. Neither of the pair had yet seen her. Claudette laughed at something Richard said, and then gazed up at him in what looked like adoration.

Richard leaned in, wanting to make sure Juliana's sister heard him. "Like I said, Claudette, even the squirrels have a purpose in God's kingdom."

She laughed, a rich throaty sound, like her sister's. "Do I look like a squirrel?"

"No." He rubbed his chin and then placed his foot on a nearby stump. "What I'm saying is, although you're not able to stand all day in the kitchen, you've been a great help, and we're happy to keep you on."

"Happy?" Her coy tone sent skitters of apprehension though him.

Oh my, he better get this back on track right quick. "Well, of course—the men love your desserts the best, and the way to get a shanty boy to work harder is to feed him well."

"Oh pooh." She bent her head back over her bowl of carrots. "What about Sven? Is he happy I'm here?"

A whoosh of sound escaped Richard's lips before he could stop it. She looked up, alarm tightening her pretty features.

"Sven is...well..." Maybe he should leave it to Sven to say he was engaged to Ruth—a sweetheart of a girl. She should be arriving soon, with her little sisters, and possibly her father.

"He's the most handsome man I've ever seen."

"Yes, well handsome is as handsome does." One of Ma's favorite expressions. This was not the way to start off a new camp; with his assistant camp manager pursued by Claudette Beauchamps.

"Hello there!" Juliana's voice carried false cheerfulness that set his jaw muscle jumping. He turned around to face her, smiling. But her smile was the fake one that she fixed on her face for difficult patrons of the library. What had he done now to deserve this expression of irritation?

She'd almost joined them, when Richard spied Dr. Adams-Payne entering the men's bunkhouse. He needed to catch the man before their part-time camp doctor headed back to Newberry. The man had a habit of lighting out of the camp before Richard could converse with him. "Excuse me, I have to talk with the doc."

He caught up with him, wanting to hurry the physician, so he could get back to Juliana. "Doc, what do you think of the conditions here? Everything look good to you?"

This was the largest and newest bunkhouse they'd ever had.

"Looks hygienic enough." Adams-Payne scanned the long rows of bunks that had plenty of space between them, unlike some camps. "As long as you don't overwork the men like some of the camps do."

"I intend to run things like my Pa did, and we never had any complaints." Other than the too-close bunks, which he'd corrected in this new building. "As far as the work, we'd not had grumbling from any men who were willing to work the same as we all did."

The man, who stood a good ten inches shorter than him, looked up and smiled. "You appear to be a very physically fit specimen of a man."

"Specimen?"

He laughed. "Never mind. I meant it as a compliment. You're a healthy, strong, young man. You need to keep in mind that you'll have some men come in with ailments that don't allow them to keep your pace. Do you understand?"

"I'll keep that in mind, Doc." Richard hadn't really pondered that notion before, but it made some sense. If he set the pace and it was too fast, some of the men would either get discouraged or tire themselves out, making them prone to illness.

"Good." Dr. Adams-Payne turned to look where the Beauchamps ladies were.

"Say, would you like to come have some dinner before you head out?" Richard jerked a thumb toward the cook house.

"That would be delightful—give me a chance to see if you're serving healthy victuals, too."

"Don't know that Claudette's apple cobbler is healthy, but it sure is good. And I think I smell cherry pie, too."

They stepped out of the sawdust-strewn room and onto the clover covered ground.

"So, would you consider Miss Beauchamps your young lady, Mr. Christy?"

"I sure wish she was, Doc, but I ain't gettin' much interest from her. Could be because I need to straighten some things out between the two of us." Such as that he'd never said he wasn't interested in courting her. If she got wind of that, who knew what she might do. On the other hand, he didn't need her getting any of Jo's misinformation that the two of them had an understanding.

The man tugged at his elbow and they stopped. "You're her employer, you should watch yourself. Miss Claudette Beauchamps has some frailties, as you surely comprehend. And is in no position to fend off..."

Richard raised his hands in surrender. "No, ya got the wrong one—Miss Juliana is a librarian for the city of St. Ignace." He dropped his arms to his sides.

"Ah." The doctor adjusted his tie and then his hat. What had him so rattled? "Her sister is a fetching young woman, despite her tart tongue."

"She's the sweetest natured gal I've met around these parts. You've formed the wrong perception."

Dr. Adams-Payne fixed a look on him. "Must I also conduct a mental examination with you, Mr. Christy?"

Richard laughed. "That gal has only been feisty with one person that I know of—and that is you, Doc."

"I see." Adams-Payne twitched into a smile. "I hope you'll provide adequate protection for her."

"Of course." He didn't need to be told to attend to a lady's needs. He'd taken good care of Jo and had helped save Rebecca. Richard clenched and then released his fists.

They strode on in silence, the doctor's eyes fixed ahead on the two young women. Or was his gaze focused on one blonde woman?

Richard gestured toward the doctor. "Juliana and Claudette, I believe you've met the doc before."

Dr. Adams-Payne nodded at Juliana and then bent over Claudette and took her hand in his. He bowed deeply, as their elderly camp driver, Frenchie, might do if he was there. Then Adams-Payne pressed a kiss to Claudette's hand. "Enchanted, Miss Beauchamps, to see you again."

Her face reddened, highlighting a butterfly-like pattern that crossed her nose, connecting both cheeks. The physician straightened, but then leaned back in.

"May I?" He placed a hand near her face.

Claudette pressed a hand to her cheeks. "Oh, no, is it there again?"

"The telltale rash, yes. I've seen this before, young lady." The doctor sat next to her. "Why are you sitting out here? Are you fatigued?"

"No, I..." She exhaled a puff of air. "Yes, I am, but I'm so much better than I was."

He turned to face Juliana. "How have her symptoms been?"

"Ask her." Juliana pointed back to Claudette. "My younger sister is twenty-four-years-old and quite capable of explaining her condition to you herself."

Nearby, men rolled wheelbarrows filled with lilac bushes past them. Juliana waited with bated breath. Would Richard notice?

The camp boss stuck his thumb and forefinger in his mouth and whistled loudly, before stomping off after the men. "What do ya think yer doin'?"

A tawny-hair youth glanced in her direction. "Lilac bushes to put in."

"Says who?" Richard barked. She'd never seen him so angry, and Juliana shrank into herself, trembling.

Sven jogged over to them. "Ja, what's wrong, boss?"

"Who in tarnation got such a fool idea in their head?" Richard's accusation made her head throb. Obviously, he'd not remembered what had been shared in the privacy of his cabin—that lilacs were her favorite flower—and that she'd not be living anywhere they didn't thrive.

Claudette cast her a look of sympathy.

"Miss Beauchamps brought them out."

"Well, she can take them right back home." Richard lowered his head and stomped off toward the men's barracks.

She would not cry. Would not. Still, one defiant tear trickled down her cheek and she swiped it away.

"Juliana, come tell Dr. Adams-Payne about your trip to Milwaukee." Claudette waved her over. "Perhaps he can prescribe something to settle your stomach."

If only that would cure what ailed her.

Chapter 12

The medication Dr. Adams-Payne had given Juliana was wearing off as the ship entered Milwaukee's inner harbor. Pink and orange washed the skies over Lake Michigan, as the sun sank lower on the horizon. If Richard were there, he'd point out how spectacular the sunset was, but all Juliana could think of was how close they now were to solid ground.

"Juliana?" Gracie lowered herself into the chair beside her on deck. "Are you feeling better now?"

"Much better." She'd slept in a small cabin for most of the trip. Sister Mary Lou yet remained in her room, having complained of stomach pain, and she'd still not risen from her narrow bunk.

Her friend stretched her arms overhead. Good thing Sister Mary Lou had stitched Gracie up new ensembles for this trip, because otherwise the young woman's blouse would have torn. It was nice to see Gracie dressed in clothing that flattered her instead of in cast offs. "I'm tired, too, but this journey has been so exhilarating!"

James Yost strolled back from the bow, his jaunty straw hat making him appear younger. "Exhilarating for you, maybe, but not for our captain, Miss Gracie, who worked hard during that storm off of Escanaba." But he laughed, grabbed the rail, and tipped his head back.

Juliana's stomach still roiled at the recollection of the high waves they'd encountered on the trip. But after the showers and turbulence, the calm arrived and, with it, fresh air.

A crisp breeze continued until the boat neared the docks. Then the crew stepped up their maneuvering. Juliana and Gracie ducked back into the cabin. Ropes groaned, steam hissed, and metal screeched for almost a half hour.

"I can't rest with all that noise." Gracie made a face when an incoming ship blasted their horn in greeting.

Juliana gently nudged Sister Mary Lou's shoulder. "You'll need to get up soon."

The nun groaned. "I don't feel well. I'm so sorry."

Gracie pressed a hand to Sister Mary Lou's forehead. "You have a little fever."

Juliana felt, too. "This might not be sea sickness, after all." But she hoped it was.

Their friend rolled away from them, threw off her covers, and pulled herself to sitting. "I'll be all right."

She and Gracie exchanged a long glance. Sister Mary Lou's recent ennui, so uncommon for her, was the reason they'd wanted her to accompany them and was why Father Paul had agreed. Was she more ill than they'd feared?

"There, I'm up." When the nun turned to face them, she had her habit adjusted and her face would have looked completely composed, had it not been for the tightness around her eyes. She was in pain.

At her first private opportunity, Juliana would share this information with Mr. Yost.

A rap at the door preceded James Yost's call. "We're ready ladies."

"Can you check and be sure we've not left anything?" She asked the others, as she grabbed her pocketbook and her overnight bag intent upon slipping outside.

As the other two women looked over the compartment, Juliana departed their cabin. "Mr. Yost?"

"Yes?" If only his handsome face, his crooked smile, and his personality appealed to her more...

"I fear Sister Mary Lou may be ill."

"Yes, I'm aware." As a gust of wind threatened to steal his hat, he clamped a hand over it. "That's one reason she's with us."

"Oh?" Was he apprised of something she hadn't been? "She seems worse."

At this, he frowned and puffed out his cheeks in a long exhalation. "My personal physician is at the hospital today, but I can have him called over to the house after dinner. Can it wait until then?"

"I believe so. I hope so."

"Thank you for alerting me, Juliana."

When she frowned, he touched her sleeve. "I hope you don't mind me calling you by your Christian name, but we'll be working closely together." He offered a warm smile.

She bobbed her head and opened the cabin door. "Ready?"

The other two women joined her and Yost. He smiled at Sister Mary Lou and offered his blue-suited arm to her. "May I accompany you down?"

"Why thank you."

"Wait for me here, ladies."

When he returned, Mr. Yost took her hand and escorted her down the ramp then returned for Gracie, who chattered nervously on the way down and then clung to Yost for a moment. "I'm dizzy. Sorry."

Concern danced over his handsome features and he led her assistant to a nearby bench and then sat down beside her, still holding her hands. Could it be? As she watched, chills coursed down her arms. Gracie was falling for James and if she was right, the feeling may be mutual. She almost chuckled out loud. *Silly me—thinking he was romantically interested in me when he's done nothing but pursue me to ask questions about libraries. Lord, is this the answer you have for Gracie?*

Sister Mary Lou paced near the water, which had turned a deeper blue. The magenta-streaked sky surrounded a sinking orange sun, as it reflected its mighty orb on the great lake. The nun moved to a black iron fence and leaned against it. The spiky tops of the fence appeared incongruous in their jutting spears against the peaceful sunset.

Nearby, an enormous, heavily gilded, black carriage pulled onto a semi-circle drive, adjacent to the harbor. Once the vehicle stopped, a door opened and a girl exited and ran toward them, her blonde hair streaming behind her. As she neared, Yost stood. "Isabelle!"

"Papa!" She launched herself into his arms.

"My dear, what are you doing here?"

"Cook said I could." She kissed Yost twice on both cheeks and then they pressed their noses together.

He turned to face Juliana and Gracie. "Ladies, this is my beautiful daughter, Isabelle."

The child curtseyed.

"And this is Miss Beauchamps, the librarian I've raved to you about. The very best librarian I've ever met." The expression in his eyes was clear to Juliana now—it was an appreciation that had nothing to do with her sex.

"Nice to meet you, Isabelle."

Yost's eyes grew softer as he turned toward Gracie. "And this is Miss Gracie, Miss Beauchamps' assistant—a lovely and sweet young lady."

"I've already told your Papa that I'd be happy to read you all the stories you want at bedtime!" Gracie clutched her hands at her waist and rocked side to side in her new kid leather pumps.

When had Yost told Gracie that he had a child? This information came as a shock to Juliana. Isabelle appeared to be about six years old, but her deportment suggested she could be older—or she was precocious.

From behind them, Sister Mary Lou cleared her throat.

"This is Sister Mary Lou, who is to chaperone these fair ladies—but who also needs a rest herself." Yost's complexion paled slightly. "And we're going to invite my friend, Dr. Howerter, to come meet her after dinner."

The child ran to her. "Are you a real nun?"

Sister Mary Lou laughed. "Yes, I am, dear."

"We go to a church that some say is as big as a cathedral in Europe." Isabelle opened her arms wide. "Have you been to one of the Catholic cathedrals there?"

"Why yes, I have."

Both Juliana and Gracie swiveled in their friend's direction. Obviously there were things she didn't know about her friends. As her assistant, Gracie had run interference for her with Mr. Yost. Had she developed an affection for the man? And now Juliana learned Sister Mary Lou had traveled to Europe. Would this trip help her learn more about herself, as well? Such as why her heart longed to be nearer to Richard Christy? She rubbed her arms. Couldn't she even be open and honest with herself? She wanted more than an invitation to The Lumberjacks' Ball. His reaction to her lilacs had stymied her. Mr. Hatchens, too, had divulged overhearing Richard's pronouncement, at the banquet, that he was not courting her. Shouldn't that disclosure have killed what feelings she'd developed for the lumberjack?

Sister Mary Lou groaned in pain and clutched her side. Juliana and Gracie went to her and Isabelle ran to her father, terror, out of proportion to the situation, washing her tiny face. What had the little girl gone through when her mother died? And could this doctor help Juliana's friend?

Sven shoved Richard's shoulder as he sat down next to him in the cookhouse. "How can I work for someone who is such a *dumhuvud*?"

Richard slid over on the bench. "Huh?"

"Sven just called you a dunce." Swede, sitting across the table, glanced between the two of them.

"Ja, are you going to fight me now?" Sven elbowed him.

Richard shook his head. "Nah, you're right." As he dug into his roast pork and potatoes, he sensed the other men's eyes on him. Richard's idiocy likely drove Juliana right into James Yost's open arms.

"You sick, boss?" Swede laid his rough cloth napkin down.

"Stop calling me boss, we've been friends for too long." Richard rested his elbows on the table, knowing what his mother would say if she were here to view him performing this "crime" in manners.

"Ja, well, I can't call you any of the other names we have said over the years." Sven laughed. "And since you don't want us calling you Moose anymore, boss is easier to say than Richard."

"No matter. When all the men return, I'll still be Moose." If only he was still someone's Bon Jean, as Juliana sometimes slipped and called him. He stifled a chuckle. The little lady imagined him the lumberjack hero of so many stories. One day someone would write those tales down and put them in a book. But it wouldn't be Richard, although he loved good storytelling.

Sven tapped at Richard's elbow. "Watch out. One of those Beauchamps ladies might find a wooden spoon and teach you some manners."

He straightened.

Swede grunted. "He must be sick. And the new doc isn't here."

"Ja, he's love sick, like his pa said." Sven pushed half a biscuit into his mouth and then chased it down with coffee.

"If ye mean over that golden-haired gal, I ken ye better give up." Scotty McNear tugged at his faded red, almost pink, suspenders and lowered his eyebrows as he met Richard's gaze across the table. "The doc has her in his sights and she's a good-looking lass, ain't she?"

"*Inte hennes.*" Sven intoned.

"Not her?" Swede grabbed a biscuit from the basket.

"Miss Juliana Beauchamps, the librarian." Richard cleared his throat. "That's who Sven's talking about, and yes, I'm a complete dunce." Pride had kept him from explaining how he couldn't tolerate lilacs in his camp.

Scotty speared a potato just as Sven reached for it, barely missing stabbing him. "Ye got the manners of a polecat— tryin' to nab my victuals from me. Dinna ken ye can take my food from me, ye young whelp."

Richard wiped his mouth and splayed his fingers open at the men. "Don't even think about starting up this fight, again, at this camp. I'll make you two sit at separate tables, like Pa used to do with me and Ox."

After slicing the large potato in a stabbing motion, Scotty plunged the knife into half and set it onto Sven's plate. "There ye be, lad."

No one but Scotty ever tried to get Sven's goat. Maybe because the big man could crush anyone who tried, if he ever got angry, which he rarely did.

Mrs. Beauchamps, her silver hair glistening beneath the kerosene lamps, brought a large bowl of stewed turnips, smothered in butter, to the table. "Here you go, men."

"Thank you, ma'am." Swede smiled up at her, grabbed the bowl and then passed it to Sven, avoiding Scotty's outstretched palms.

The wooden bowl, elaborately decorated with carved and painted cherries, wasn't one Richard had brought for the camp. Juliana's mother followed his narrowed gaze. "That's one of mine, Mr. Christy, from home."

"Pretty thing." Sven rotated it slowly, admiring the handiwork.

Ox could make something similar. An idea sparked the dead wood in Richard's dunderhead. "Sven, I'll be going to Mackinac Island tomorrow first thing. Gotta see my brother."

There was more than one way to bring lilacs into this camp. What would his cabin look like with a pretty lilac painted chest for Juliana? A rocker with lilac blossoms carved into the back? And surely at one of those fancy art shops on Mackinac Island, he'd find a painting of lilacs that they could hang on the wall. His spirits rose for the first time since she'd departed. But was he too late?

The Yost carriage rolled to a stop near a three story tan brick building whose façade was embellished in a gingerbread style, with a jagged edge covering the top level, beneath the steep tile roof. A herringbone brick walkway bisected the rolling lawn. Thankfully, Sister Mary Lou's symptoms were calming. But Juliana wanted to get her friend right to bed.

"I thought you might like to enter from the front instead of the side—give you a chance to get your land legs again." Mr. Yost gave her a meaningful gaze. He obviously had the same thoughts she had, wanting to get them in as quickly as possible. He assisted the nun out rather than waiting on his footman.

He called up to the driver and footman, "Bring the trunks in and have Rawley bring them upstairs. Sister Mary Lou's first, please. Let Maisy direct where the others should go."

"No, Papa!" His daughter hopped down into his arms. "I want to show them."

"All right then, peanut." He kissed her forehead and she ran across the lawn as a slender, dark-suited man opened one of the massive paneled front doors.

Soon Juliana and Gracie stepped down from the carriage, assisted by Mr. Yost. He offered his arm to Sister Mary Lou.

"Mr. Yost, I am fine now. You mustn't baby me. I'll be quite all right once I've rested." Sister Mary Lou was standing straighter now, and the color had returned to her wan cheeks.

"I pray you will be."

"I'm sure I shall—once I've rested."

He turned to address Juliana. "I can hardly wait for you to see the plans I have for the new library."

She forced a smile. "That's why we're here."

Mr. Yost quirked an eyebrow at her. "I've invited my personal assistant to join us for dinner tomorrow night—rather, he's my former personal secretary. Alek has had a promotion. He's assumed more responsibilities at my brewery."

Alek. That was the nickname she'd given Aleksanteri so many years ago. "I look forward to meeting him." And Alek now lived in Milwaukee. *Surely not. Oh Lord, please.*

"We'll have a little repast tonight after we get you settled in your rooms."

She had to move quickly to keep up with his long strides but he didn't slow for her, as Richard always did.

"That would be lovely. Between Sister Mary Lou's stomach problems, my fear of the ship, and Gracie's fascination with the water, I fear none of us has gotten much food down today."

He laughed. "Gracie was born for the waves." The affection in his voice gave her pause. Was the man falling in love with her assistant? But of greater concern right now was Sister Mary Lou and this Alek, whom he'd mentioned.

Juliana ran her tongue over her lower lip. "Your former assistant, Alek, you said. It's not Alex or Alexander?"

His features bunched in concentration. "No, it is Alek. I never could pronounce his name but it's not Alexander."

"What is his last name?"

"Puumala." He grinned, as though he'd won a prize. "I can pronounce that name. Why do you ask?"

She gritted her teeth. "It would be best if you do not invite him quite yet, sir. I can explain later, in private."

"You know Mr. Puumala then?"

Perspiration broke out on her forehead. This trip was turning into the nightmare she'd feared it could be, although not in the ways she'd imagined and discussed with her sister. "Let's leave it at that."

A dark-suited man held the door. "Welcome back, sir," he greeted Mr. Yost warmly.

Yost handed him his boater, and his light coat, and then gestured for the women to pass their coats to his servant.

Gracie entered first and stood staring, gape-mouthed until Sister Mary Lou joined her and whispered something. Having seen pictures of Yost's mansion in one of the library books about Milwaukee, Juliana thought she'd be prepared for its opulence, but she wasn't. Even after the shock of learning Yost was Alek's employer, Juliana had to force her lips to remain together as she scanned the gargantuan entryway. Black and white marble floor tiles alternated in a diagonal pattern. An almost six-foot-wide chandelier, hanging high overhead, dangled thousands of crystals. To the right, a man-sized gilded baroque mirror hung on the burgundy flocked wallpapered walls. A cherrywood umbrella stand stood to the right, and a mahogany coat rack to the left, presumably for temporary guests, because the manservant carried their summer coats to a nearby closet.

Ahead, a teal carpeted staircase wound at a steep curve up to the second level. Portraits of dour-looking European-dressed men from times past, presumably Yost's ancestors, covered the adjacent wall. The overall effect was rather daunting. Juliana swallowed hard.

"Meet me back down in the parlor in a half hour, ladies." Mr. Yost gestured to the left, where a sitting room was visible through open paneled walnut pocket doors. A red velvet settee with curved cabriole legs hugged the wall with two rose-colored wing chairs facing it. Four black leather upholstered wooden chairs surrounded a claw-footed cherrywood card table.

The grandfather clock that she'd passed chimed and echoed in the foyer.

Isabelle entered the room from a hallway that connected further down the expansive room. "Come on, everyone!"

A red-haired woman hastily followed her, her apron flapping away from her dark skirt. "Welcome home, Mr. Yost."

"Glad to be here, Maisy. Can you help our guests up to their rooms?"

"Papa, that's my job." Isabelle rolled her eyes.

Juliana chuckled and Gracie moved forward to take the child's hand. "Won't you please show us our rooms?"

As they mounted the stairs, the cushioned carpet sank beneath Juliana's feet. What luxury. When they reached the top, the little girl opened the first paneled door on the right, in the hallway, and slid the pocket door into the wall. Gracie squealed in delight. "This is the room we'll share?"

A four-poster double bed, covered in lilac silk bedding, predominated the room's center. Beyond, in a small alcove, nestled a single bed, presumably for a lady's maid.

Maisy's cheeks reddened. "Oh no, miss. You'll each have your own rooms and a maid, if you wish, to attend you."

Isabelle climbed up the two steps of the small wooden structure beside the bed, and onto it. "Papa said this bed might be too high for Miss Juliana. He said you were petite. I like that word."

Juliana's mouth twitched into a smile. But her humor vanished when her companion gasped in pain.

Sister Mary Lou's face drained of color and she sank into a padded boudoir chair. Perspiration beaded on her brow and Juliana rushed to her. "Are you all right?"

"Just tired."

This was more than fatigue. "Miss, um, Maisy, could you please show us to Sister Mary Lou's bedchamber right away?" And they'd need to get the physician.

"Yes'm." Maisy dipped into a brief curtsy.

"And Gracie, could you stay here with Isabelle, and have her tell you about the house?"

"Yes," the child answered for Gracie. "I'll be the bestest hostess Papa has had yet."

The servant led them next door. "Here you are."

"Thank goodness," her friend sighed and pointed to the low bed.

Maisy rushed to the bed, and pulled back the ivory matelassé coverlet. Sister Mary Lou immediately laid down, habit and all.

"You're not well, Sister." The servant began removing Sister Mary Lou's shoes. "I think we'd best get you undressed and into bed."

"Let me help." Juliana clutched her hands, wanting to do something, anything, to ease the nun's distress. "And would you please go to Mr. Yost and have him send for the doctor?"

"Yes'm."

Sister Mary Lou groaned. Juliana went to her and began helping the nun out of her heavy clothing.

"No, no, I can do it myself." But when the nun struggled to sit up and couldn't, Juliana patted her hand.

"Lie still. You are clearly unwell. Be a good patient for me."

Although clearly embarrassed, Sister Mary Lou permitted her to remove her garments until she was clad in what looked like a very long slip.

Maisy soon returned. "Mr. Yost already sent for the doctor. He's such a good man." The latter reference seemed to apply to her employer.

Isabelle bounded into the room, but then stopped. "Oh no. You're not going to die like my momma did, are you?" Tears sprang to her eyes.

Stepping between the child and the nun, Maisy shook her head. "No, lass."

But were the child's words correct? How many people had Mother ministered to, over the years, as they lay dying from peritonitis? *Dear God, please…*

Chapter 13

Wheels rumbled toward the office, a little too fast for Richard's liking.

Avery Bell emitted a low whistle. "Now there's a handsome woman." The rural mail route carrier's daughter drove her carriage straight toward them, and Richard pushed Avery out of the way as the woman cut a little too close.

When she finally brought her horses to a halt, half of her chestnut brown curls tumbled free from beneath her wide-brimmed straw hat. "Gentlemen?"

Bell grinned up at her like a puppy awaiting a treat. "Miss Griffis?"

"Mr. Bell." Her pert nose tipped up. "My father is ill, so I'm carrying his route again today."

Carrying? More like rampaging across the countryside with it. But with Miss Griffis toting the mail for her father, they kept the income in the family.

Richard rubbed his chin. "Miss Griffis, can ya give me a few minutes to go grab our outgoing mail?"

"Certainly."

A grin split the handyman's face. "I bet Mr. Christy wouldn't mind if I showed you around his new camp while you're waiting, would you, eh?" He turned to Richard.

Richard ducked his chin in agreement.

Miss Griffis batted her eyelashes at Avery. "You might wish to ask *me*, Mr. Bell."

Removing his hat, Bell bent at the waist and then made a sweeping gesture. "Milady, may I have the honor of escorting you through this fair village, our new lumber camp?"

She stifled a giggle. "It has to be quick, I still have mail to deliver."

The lady, judging from her appearance, had to be a good five to ten years Bell's junior. But what did that matter in God's timing? Might be good for Avery to hitch up again. Did Juliana trouble herself about such trifling matters? He'd add a line about that very matter in his letter to her.

"Go on, Avery, and show Miss Griffis around while I get the letters to go out."

The brunette handed Richard a twine-bound bundle of correspondence. "That's all the camp's mail."

"Thank you, ma'am."

After tucking the mail under his arm, Richard strode across the spongy, sandy, soil to his cabin. Once inside, he pushed his stack of Ox-personalized plaques out of the way. Hopefully, Juliana would appreciate the significance of the lilacs carved into them. A grin tugged at his mouth as he imagined her reaction. Then he scowled, imagining the ribbing he'd take when the lumberjacks saw the camp buildings labeled with lilac-embellished signs. He sat at his makeshift desk, a tall one with a good-sized chair Moose had constructed. Now if only his brother's and Rebecca's encouraging words and prayers were effective.

Locating his fountain pen, he drew up the ink, and then added a line to his note. Then he pushed the love letter aside, to make sure the ink was dry before sealing it. While his words may not be wonderfully poetic, they were the best he could put together. And his apology was heartfelt, that was for sure.

He retrieved his letter opener from the wooden desk organizer that Ox had made for him, grinning at the fancy lilacs carved into the wood. What if Juliana didn't accept his offer? What if his concerns about Yost were valid? He'd sure have quite the collection of lilac-decorated furnishings for his cabin and the camp.

He cut the twine. On top were two bills from town and a *carte de visite* picture postcard from Kentucky, featuring his aunt and his cousins sitting in front of their cabin. The fourth piece of mail was a letter addressed to Claudette, in her sister's beautiful handwriting. What was that doing here? It was addressed to her home. Maybe Miss Griffis knew Juliana's sister would be at the camp. Postmark was Milwaukee. Richard set it down. His fingers itched to open it, but he pushed it aside. The next letter was for Juliana's mother, also with a return address at Yost's mansion. Who was Richard kidding? Why would Juliana want to come back to him? To a lumber camp? He snorted in disgust at himself. *God, I believe in miracles and this here situation is gonna need one.*

He continued through the rest of the stack, hoping to see something from Juliana for him. The bottom letter's ink was so smeared that Miss Griffis must have eagle's eyes to have made out the address and name. Had the storms in Wisconsin damaged the mail? The ships that had come into port held passengers complaining of the rough weather they'd been having. Must be Milwaukee got its fair share of rain, because only those letters had sullied ink. He could discern only a few letters on the name, but the Milwaukee postmark was clear. He opened it, his heart beating.

My dear one,

She thought him dear? The Lord was indeed answering prayers.

More smears on the letter made it hard to decipher. Must have had downpours over there for the rain to have penetrated clear through to the paper inside. Or had Juliana been crying when she'd written it?

I fear for Sister Mary Lou's life. By the time you read this she may have died.

His gut clenched as he scanned ahead, but Richard couldn't make out the writing in the rest of the blurred paragraph. What had happened? The nun had been tired out from all her exertions for the orphans, but when he'd last seen her, she'd been excited about the trip.

Too many deceptions have been wrought on me and I fear...

Once again the words disappeared into the paper. Richard leaned as close to the letter as he could but he couldn't read what it said. But then another distinct sentence loomed.

My dear sister, pray do not tell Richard.

This letter was for Claudette? He should stop reading, but he had to know.

A rat-a-tat-tat knock on the door preceded Sven's entrance. "Father Paul is here with Reverend Jones. Come on out, now, ja? I think you better talk with the priest. He's very upset."

As was Richard. He handed Sven the letters for Mrs. Beauchamps and Claudette. "Bring these to them, would ya." Why had both clergymen come out if only one was upset?

Reverend Jones nodded to Richard, but kept his distance, standing near his carriage and feeding carrots to his two bay mares.

Father Paul paced in the clearing, his shiny shoes kicking up dust that would surely coat them if he didn't stop. "Mr. Christy. We must converse."

"Is it about Sister Mary Lou?" Richard swallowed back a lump in his throat.

The man's eyes widened. "What do you mean? I'm here because of Gracie."

Richard puffed out a breath of air. "Sir, Father Paul, that is..."

"Do you have word from them?"

"Sister Mary Lou is very ill." Richard shoved a hand back through his hair as his lips curled around the words he was about to say. "She may be dying, if Juliana's letter is correct."

Color drained from the priest's face. He tugged at his clerical collar. Richard pointed toward a bench by the cook house. The savory scents emerging from within couldn't tease the sour feeling in Richard's gut as the man slumped onto the bench.

The two Beauchamps women exited the wooden structure and hastened to them, their skirts swishing rapidly.

Mrs. Beauchamps went to the priest's side. "Are you all right, Father Paul?"

"I'm worried." He tugged at his collar. "Which is one reason Reverend Jones drove me straight out."

"We're worried, too." Claudette waved her letter. "Why, I believe that Mr. Yost may be a wicked man."

Mrs. Beauchamps grabbed Claudette's free hand. "I fear the same thing. Dishonest at the very least."

Sun touched Claudette's golden hair, giving her an angelic appearance, as though she'd been sent to deliver a message to them. "From what Juliana wrote, that beer baron's house could be straight out of a gothic novel—a terrifying one." She shivered.

The priest pressed a hand to his chest. "Lord, forgive me. What have I sent those two into?"

Didn't he mean three, not two? Did the priest only have concern for his nun and the orphan under his care? What about Juliana? What about her predicament? And it was Richard's fault. He should have put aside his vanity and accepted what everyone, including his sister, Jo, had explained. Juliana was offering herself as his wife—the lilacs being a symbolic gesture of her affection for him and willingness to live with him. But he wasn't one for understanding symbolic stuff— give it to him straight any day. Still, he'd gotten it now and he had lilac-decorated items coming, enough to fill up his entire cottage.

Mrs. Beauchamps' eyes filled with tears. "What have you heard, Father Paul?"

"Actually, it was Reverend Jones who received communication." He pulled an envelope from his pocket and passed it to her. "Mrs. Puumula, Alek's mother, brought this in to him, she was so concerned. It says that since the women have arrived, James Yost doesn't allow them out of the house."

Claudette gasped. "Just like a Gothic villain would do. I just knew it."

Richard rubbed his jaw.

The priest nodded, solemnly. "Furthermore, they're not accepting visitors. Mr. Yost is isolating them and Aleksanteri was worried enough that he wrote to his mother."

"For Alek to write his mother about this situation, he has to be dreadfully afraid." Mrs. Beauchamps dabbed at tears in her eyes. "My poor girl. Even that boy who broke off their engagement is concerned."

Richard's heartbeat sped up.

"Aleksanteri pointed out that, like Yost's wife, Sister Mary Lou was taken to the hospital with abdominal pains."

"Do you think he may have killed his own wife?" Claudette raised her hands to cover her mouth.

Although Yost didn't seem the evil-doer type, for a man to write his ma about a former sweetheart didn't bode well.

"He didn't say his opinion, but reading between the lines, it sounds as though Aleksanteri Puumala fears so. And he'd heard they had a beautiful young woman at the mansion, who Yost may intend to press into marriage."

Juliana. His Juliana. Forced to marry Yost? Had he forced his attentions on her? Heat crawled up his neck.

Claudette dropped her hands to her side. "Just like one of those gothics where the demented man locks an innocent young woman up in the attic. Maybe he even killed his wife. Maybe she didn't die of natural causes."

"And now Sister Mary Lou is deathly ill." Richard tried to maintain composure, but his breath seemed to stick in his throat. "The very person who is supposed to be chaperoning the younger women."

Richard swallowed back his fears. He had to take action. All around him, in camp, readiness for the lumberjacks was moving forward. This place would be nothing to him if he didn't have Juliana with him. But did she love him? He loved her so much he'd endure years of teasing about lilacs in the lumber camp—decorating everything from camp signage to their biscuit bowls. Yet, Juliana hadn't sent him any mail.

Pushing a silver strand of hair behind her ear, Juliana's mother displayed her own letter. "My daughter is desperately unhappy. And while she's always been straightforward in what she tells me, in this missive, she seems to be beating around the bush about something. It's the strangest thing." She nibbled on her lower lip. "I'm her mother. She should be able to tell me she loves me. Why would she include so many poetic phrases that allude to her affection rather than writing it." Tears rolled down her cheeks.

Claudette sat next to her mother and grasped the older woman's hands.

Hope sprang in Richard's heart.

"Mind if I take a gander at that note, ma'am?" Richard held out a hand.

She passed it to him and sniffed. "I'm worried that she's coming unraveled. I'd heard she may lose her job here. I know she enjoys her work, but I wonder if this position is causing her great stress and confusion. Or could it be Mr. Yost is the cause of her trouble?"

"There may be another explanation, Mrs. Beauchamps." Richard unfolded the letter and scanned the greeting first. "Yup, it got wet, like mine did. But I can see Dear and the first letter."

That was an "R" and not an "M" for mother. Dear Richard—not Dear Mother. He'd read this in private, later. A grin twitched at his lips, which fought to scowl at the situation Yost had put his beloved in. "Mind if I keep this for now?"

Three pairs of eyes fixed on him.

The side door to the kitchen opened and Melanie emerged, her children clustered around her. "I could use some help in here!"

"Coming." Claudette rose and pulled her mother to standing.

Richard frowned. "Father Paul, would you come and pray with me?"

The priest stood, motioned for Reverend Jones, and the two clergymen followed Richard to his cabin.

God, what is your will in this situation? He almost sensed the Lord telling him to just use his head. And his heart. Father Paul and Reverend Jones each took a seat. As Richard pulled his chair from the desk, he focused on the last legible line in Juliana's letter to her sister, which he'd begun reading earlier.

I think if Richard heard this news, he'd abandon his camp and come bring us home.

James, as he'd insisted she call him and finally had, appeared immaculate in a navy suit jacket and cuffed trousers, as he rolled Sister Mary Lou, in a wheelchair, into the Yost library. The man always managed to look handsome, no matter what he wore—as did Richard, even in a checked flannel shirt. Did her Bon Jean miss her?

Juliana went to her and gave the nun a hug. "I'm so glad you're back, Sister Mary Lou."

"Not as happy as I am, I can assure you!"

Grinning, James met her gaze. "I wanted to bring her in here to see what you're working on, Juliana. Then I'm getting her right back *ins Bett*—to bed—doctor's orders."

Sister Mary Lou's eyes widened as she scanned the room. The personal library, situated in the south turret of the house, featured mullioned windows spanning eight feet and towering ten feet high. Multiple woods, in the furnishings, warmed the room. The oak desk, cherrywood table and chairs, dark mahogany filing cabinets, and light ash built-in book cases blended well with the multi-colored Persian wool rug that covered the pine floor. "Mr. Yost's private library will be the envy of every Milwaukee citizen."

"I agree." Juliana had worked hard on bringing order to the collection, but it was Yost's own vision that had made the library in his home such a welcoming place.

"Thank you, ladies."

Her friend winced, as though in pain.

"Are you all right?" Juliana cringed. They'd prayed that the nun was now past any possible infection.

"Yes, I'm fine. The physician warned me I'd have some pain."

"And that you'd be on bed rest for some time to come. I'm afraid I got overzealous." James carefully maneuvered the wheelchair in an arc in the center of the turret. "Time for a rest, Sister Mary Lou."

Juliana bent and kissed her friend's soft cheek, inhaling the scent of harsh hospital soap. She'd make sure Etta or Lela helped the nun with a sponge bath that included some of Juliana's own Pears soap.

Despite pushing a wheelchair, James appeared more relaxed than he had been in weeks. "I'll be back in a few moments to discuss our social calendar, now that this precious lady is home from the hospital."

Isabelle skipped through the tower entrance, toward them. "Let me help push."

Yost made a show of stepping aside to allow his daughter to place her hands on the handles and walk before him—with him actually doing the heavy work. Juliana grinned. The man had turned out to be quite a surprise to her. Although she didn't agree with his methods, and she was concerned about his attention toward Gracie, she was thankful James Yost had not pressed Juliana into revealing more about her relationship with Alek. And she could tell he was curious about her relationship with his former personal secretary. She'd shared that she and Aleksanteri had been "close friends", which had been true, and that she positively did not wish to see him.

With Sister Mary Lou's emergency surgery for appendicitis over, and her recovering to continue at the Yost mansion, no doubt James expected for them to accept visitors. *How could that be a good idea?*

Chapter 14

Juliana returned to ordering the books and creating labels to affix to the spines. The Ingraham chiming gingerbread clock announced the hour as James returned.

He drew near and reached for a copy of *Little Men*. "I'd like to have Mr. Puumala over. You'd like the man Alek has become."

"I'd hope so." Not that she cared to see him.

Beaming, her temporary employer tapped a crate of books. "All Horatio Alger volumes."

"I'm not surprised." She grinned up at him. "He's your favorite."

"Indeed, and Alek is a bootstrap boy, like Alger's heroes."

A hero who'd abandoned his fiancée. Juliana gritted her teeth.

"He's a rising star at Yost Brewery and was the best personal assistant I've ever had." He chuckled and rubbed his chin. "But you'd not believe where I met him."

"Oh?" She really didn't care to discuss her old fiancé. Apparently now that the crisis with Sister Mary Lou was over, so was Juliana's ban on visitors.

He fixed his gaze on her. "Alek was a miner in the western end of the Upper Peninsula. Then one day, he'd come to Milwaukee with *der Kompagnon*—a companion. And he'd seen an ad and decided he'd apply for my job as personal assistant." He laughed.

The muscles in her neck tightened. "Did he have any experience?"

The sunlight puddling on the carpet dimmed. Outside, visible through the large windows, clouds loomed over the lake.

"*Himmel, nein.*"

This German phrase flummoxed her. She squeezed her eyebrows together in concentration.

He set the children's book down. "Sorry. Now that I am home, I'm more likely to slip into the tongue I was raised with, as you've discovered. And I don't always explain what I mean."

"You usually do, though." She'd noticed, but hadn't pointed it out. And he generally explained himself unless the German words were very similar to English. Maybe that was part of his stiffness in demeanor in St. Ignace—perhaps he was expending a great deal of energy ensuring he spoke only in English. When she'd gone walking, she'd heard many people speaking in German. But in her hometown it was rarely used. And some men of commerce looked down on people who didn't speak only in English.

"I was saying, *heavens no*, Alek had no experience as an executive assistant."

"But he had plenty of nerve, didn't he?" She'd forgiven him. Hadn't she?

"He had nerve aplenty and so he showed up, dressed in his working man clothes, not in a suit much less in something pressed." He tapped a book. "It was almost like having a character from one of Alger's appear from out of a book." Like Richard coming to the library and her imagining Paul Bon Jean, of the legendary stories, coming to life.

She nodded and peeked inside the next crate, which held more children's books. "Isabelle will love all these books by Miss Alcott."

"Louisa May Alcott is definitely her favorite." He removed a handful of Alger books from his crate. "Yes, Alek is a rare find—a man who rose to the occasion and he's performed admirably. I can't wait for you to see him. He seems rather agitated as to why he's not already been invited—even though I explained about Sister Mary Lou's surgery."

Agitated? Why should he wish to see her? Mortification began, as she imagined him wanting to see her in order to explain himself and to excuse his behavior. "Sounds to me as though Aleksanteri hasn't yet learned about social expectations."

"Perhaps." He arched an eyebrow at her. "But are you ready for company?"

She'd never be ready to see Alek, but she bit her lip. She couldn't wait to get back home. This whole trip seemed a travesty—James knew enough about library order to have simply hired someone local and instructed them in what to do. With his constant attentive and gallant behavior toward Gracie, it seemed James was more interested in having her assistant there rather than having a true need of Juliana's skills. With Sister Mary Lou recuperating, she needed to return home. "Now certainly isn't the time for guests. Perhaps before I leave for St. Ignace." As in, right before she boarded the boat and could hastily wave goodbye to Aleksanteri, hopefully forever.

James straightened and then slacked his hip. "You know, I had to talk him out of running back home, after he'd first arrived in Milwaukee."

"Why?" A muscle near her eye twitched. He'd wanted to return?

"Seems he'd promised a young woman that he'd marry her, and he'd set off for the mines to prove himself and make a living. Since you two were friends, you probably know all that." Thankfully he didn't look up from examining the books and sorting them or he'd see steam coming from her ears.

Juliana gritted her teeth together.

Yost continued to stack the books into piles. "But Alek didn't do well in the mines, and felt he couldn't support a wife."

After grabbing the pry bar, Juliana forced open another wooden crate of books, thankful for the relief it provided her tense muscles. She sensed James' gaze on her back.

"But after taking my position, Alek wanted to go back and see if his young lady was willing."

Was he trying to goad her? Didn't sound like it. The man sounded positively innocent in his comments.

"After all those years?" she croaked. "He sure did have some nerve, didn't he?" She swiveled slightly toward him, forcing her facial expression into a placid mask.

He cast her a quick glance but resumed unpacking the books. "Well, I told him for one thing she'd probably gotten married, but he said no, she hadn't."

No, she had not. Juliana's sound of agreement emerged like a stifled snort.

"And for another thing, I explained to him that if he was going to be a real self-made man—an Alger man—he needed to aim higher in his ambitions." He gestured to the grand room in which they worked. "Get himself a home after he works his way up at Yost Breweries. He's not yet thirty, he has time."

Not much, as he'd be thirty shortly. Had he lied to his employer about his age, like he'd deceived Juliana?

So Yost had talked her former fiancé out of coming back for her and then convinced him he needed to earn enough to support a wife in style? "Seems to me that if they were really in love, she'd not want to wait—she'd take him as he was." Even if that meant living in a lumber camp. Even with no lilacs. *Oh Richard, why haven't I heard from you?* Was he, too, waiting until he could get out of the lumbering business and build a fine house in town?

"That had occurred to me, but in truth, since Alek didn't much resist my suggestion that he find himself a wife here in Milwaukee, instead, and later, well…"

Unbidden tears leapt to her eyes. Not that she yet loved Alek, but that this man could be so interfering in the lives of others. He had behaved like the puppet master they'd sometimes had perform at the library. But Aleksanteri had chosen to play the willing marionette. She needed to get home, wanted to return, to see mother and discover what God had planned for her next.

She knew one thing for certain—Richard Christy would never be anyone's marionette. But what about her? Had she allowed herself to continue in unforgiveness, her feelings tugged by lines connecting her to Alek?

"James, that's fine—with Alek coming to dinner." And as soon as the words came out of her mouth, it really did seem fine.

"Good. I'll send for him."

"For tonight?"

"He's been hounding me, Juliana, ever since you arrived." He laughed. "I'll be glad to get him focused back on his work."

She brushed at her dusty skirt. "I believe I'll need to change."

James gestured toward the archway exit. "Take all the time you need. And I'll send Maisy up to help you and Gracie."

Not only did Maisy arrive at her room but so did Alice, one of the servants hired especially to care for the three newcomers to the household. After an hour of bathing, hair styling, and applying cosmetics, lotion and perfume, Juliana donned her undergarments only to have Maisy pull her corset so tight that she could barely breathe. "Let it out, please."

"But, miss, you have a perfect bell shaped figure with it as it is," the servant protested.

"I don't care. I won't be able to speak unless you release the tension."

The two complied, and then helped her into her slip, bustle, and then the dinner gown of sapphire blue that Gracie claimed matched her eyes exactly.

"Lovely, isn't she, Alice?"

"Indeed." The other servant adjusted the lace around the low cut neckline and gently turned her toward the baroque mirror.

The reflection could have been another person entirely. A rosy-cheek, young-looking woman, with upswept dark curls trailing down her neck peered back at her. She pressed her hand to her rouged lips.

"Bears a striking resemblance to my former mistress. And Mrs. Yost was said to be one of the greatest beauties in Milwaukee." Maisy sighed.

Was that why James had brought her there? Isabelle had shown no reaction to Juliana's appearance. But then again, Mrs. Yost likely dressed in this fine manner every day. "Will Isabelle be upset, seeing me like this? If, as you say, I resemble her mother?"

The two servants exchanged a knowing glance. "She won't be at dinner. Neither will Miss Gracie. They're taking dinner upstairs with Sister Mary Lou. Etta and Lela will be helping."

"Oh." So it would be only her, James, and Aleksanteri. Better to get this over.

She put on the ear bobs that James had given her, hoping they weren't real gemstones, although they appeared to be. Of course, she'd leave them behind when she returned home.

After they assisted her in donning the matching necklace, the servants arranged Juliana's gown for her and showed her how to loop the train material up so that she wouldn't trip on the stairs. "Better that way, miss, than us carrying it behind you as we might all trip coming down those stairs."

Halfway down the curve in the staircase, Rawley responded to a knock at the front door. She hesitated. Removing his hat, a tall blond-haired man entered. The servant took the derby hat and hung it from a nearby brass hook. She resumed her descent, stopping only when Alek took three strides into the room and stared up at her.

"Juli?" His hoarse rasp stirred her. Still as handsome as ever, even more so, his broad shoulders filled out a light gray suit jacket. Gray plaid wool cuffed pants terminated over black shoes buffed to a high gloss. His crisp white shirt was accented by a red bow tie, above which his Adam's apple seemed to bob.

Averting her gaze, heart hammering, Juliana descended the rest of the stairs. When she reached the bottom, she held out her gloved hands to him. "How are you Alek?"

This close, she could see the fine lines etched around eyes that had always fascinated her. Tonight, though, she thought she read sadness somehow combined with relief that tugged at his lips. "So, you are well?"

"I am blessed." She truly was. Finally, seeing her old beau face-to-face, she could give up her anger and disappointment.

Alek glanced to the left, where Rawley had discreetly exited to the dining room, and then to the right, where the kitchen and servants were busily preparing their meal behind closed doors. "Juli, I am so sorry. I've wanted to tell you for so long."

He raised her hands to his lips and kissed her fingers, the warmth not passing through the lacy material. Once upon a time, to hear these words would have thrilled her to her marrow. She'd have been giddy with renewed love. "I forgive you, Alek. I have a full life and no regrets."

Every word was true. A boulder of limestone lifted from her shoulders.

Footfalls hammered down the steps, as James joined them. "Ah, I'm glad you two had a moment alone to chat."

"So am I." Gratitude filled her with warmth. The past firmly behind her, she could enjoy whatever it was God had prepared for her.

Alek pressed his lips together.

"Let's go on to the dining room." James slipped his arm through hers, although not in a proprietary way. "You two have a lot to catch up on, and I'm going to enjoy hearing your stories."

She turned and caught Alek's rueful smile.

After they'd been seated at the long mahogany table, servants poured wine for the men. Then course after superb course was delivered to the table.

Between watercress salad and tomato bisque, Juliana learned that Alek had been very ill in the mines, right near the time her brother had succumbed to illness there.

"I was so very happy when Mr. Yost gave me a job as his assistant." Alek dabbed at his mouth. "I think he may have saved my life."

James raised his palm. "Tut, tut, I did no such thing. But I did find my best assistant ever."

"Thank you." Alek's cheeks flamed red.

"And Juliana, you are the best librarian I've ever met."

"Do you enjoy the work?" Strain tinged Alek's words, and possibly regret.

The desire to burst out with "what choice did I have after you left?" was squelched immediately. "As you know, it wasn't what I'd planned to do with my life."

A carved pork roast was delivered on a creamy bone china platter, and one of the servants began clearing the soup bowls while the other placed multiple slivers of meat on their plates. Meanwhile, two more vegetables dishes were brought in and set on the sideboard. All the serving activity hushed their conversation.

James immediately began cutting his pork into edible portions. "What did you wish to do?"

She and Alek locked gazes but he spoke first. "Can you believe this lovely lady…"

Juliana had to cut him off. "…once wished to be a cook in a lumber camp."

Averting his gaze, Alek chopped his meat into tiny pieces.

Her host stared at her. "What a shame that would have been."

"I thought so." A muscle in Alek's jaw jumped.

"Such a waste of a gifted mind." James reached for the butter dish, before the servant could get it for him. "Not that such work isn't useful or necessary."

"Juliana would have wasted away in a lumber camp."

She gritted her teeth. Just like Aleksanteri to always be deciding what he thought was right for her. A trait that at the time she saw as indicating a strong mind. Maybe he had something in common with Mr. Hatchens. "I'm certain you are wrong, Alek."

"Oh?" He speared a piece of asparagus, covered in hollandaise sauce, and shoved it in his mouth.

"My choice of living in a lumber camp had more to do with the people who lived there." Like him and his parents. But obviously, that was not the right place for her former fiancé.

The beer baron raised his goblet and the servant refilled it with wine. "Ah, like now, I believe. When a certain handsome lumberjack is luring you away from the library."

After Aleksanteri's crystal glass was also refilled, he cleared his throat. "So you'll end up living in a lumber camp after all?"

"If I have my way." She sipped her chilled water. Wouldn't the well water at Richard's camp taste divine after drinking city water? Juliana could already picture herself there.

But was her desire in alignment with Richard's? Or had his rejection of lilacs in his camp been his refusal of her?

Chapter 15

One week later

"Where is she?" The man in the stiff monkey suit wouldn't allow him past, so Richard lifted the butler up and moved him aside before striding into the huge foyer, floored with black and white slippery-looking marble. "Juliana!"

Yost stepped from a nearby room, a newspaper in his hands. "What are you bellowing about, Mr. Christy?" The beer baron looked toward the staircase, and in a flash, Richard mounted the curving steps, two at a time.

"Juliana!" He hollered at the top of his lungs, heart hammering. "Where are you?"

When he reached the top, he glanced left and then right, but didn't see her. Nearby movement drew his attention to a nook, straight ahead of him. A lady rose to her tiny height from a bench, a book in her hand. A young dark-haired woman emerged, her hair swooped up atop her head. There was his Juliana, dressed in a lilac-colored, fancy gown.

"Richard?" Juliana's book clattered to the floor.

Without hesitation, he swooped in, lifted her, and clutched her to his chest, then kissed her petal-soft cheeks. "Juliana, you're all right. Thank God."

"Of course I am." Tears filled her blue eyes.

"I'm not hurtin' you, am I?" He set her down.

She gazed up at him with longing in her eyes, mirroring what he felt in his heart. "What are you doing here?"

"Did you get my letter?"

She blushed. "Yes, I did. I'd despaired I'd never hear from you."

"And?" He drew her a little closer and bent his head closer, enjoying her light perfume.

A grin tugged at her mouth. "And I may have an answer for you."

He covered her soft lips with his, lost in the sensation of finally claiming her as his own. Juliana grasped his shoulders. All the pent-up fervor he'd stifled now threatened to bust loose. He pulled away.

The pupils of her eyes loomed large and dark. "Did you receive my missive, too? Is that why you're here?"

Richard swallowed. He should be more concerned about the other two ladies, but all he could think of at the moment was making sure Juliana was safe. "Is Sister Mary Lou all right?"

"She'll need at least another month before she can travel."

"Reckon she'll have to stay here, then, when we go."

"When we go?"

"Tomorrow."

She raised a dark eyebrow. "I believe that's best for Gracie. Although she is officially employed as Isabelle's nanny, now, I believe some chaperoning is still in order."

"He ain't bothered her, has he?"

Juliana chuckled. "I'm guessing there may be a wedding in this household before Sister Mary Lou departs."

"And another wedding sooner than that, if I have my way." He breathed in the sweet scent of her, wanting to pull her close again.

"Dr. Howerter recommends Sister Mary Lou return by train, not by ship." She cocked her head to the side.

"Good idea." That darned infernal ship made him seasick. He still felt a little queasy.

Juliana ran a finger over his lower lip. "So we'll return by train?"

He was never getting on another boat, again, if he could help it, but she didn't need to know that. But look what happened by not telling her about his trouble with lilacs. "Both. I ain't too keen on boat travel."

Instead of disgust, or disapproval, she clapped her hands together. "I feel the same way."

"About ships or about being in love?" He kissed her again, lifting her off her feet before slowly lowering her until her feet touched the carpet on the floor. She pressed in against him and he deepened the kiss. Lord, have mercy, there would be a batch of little Christy young'uns in no time at all once they got hitched.

Juliana groaned. She must get herself under control. She continued embracing Richard and kissing him until she heard someone clearing their throat, behind them.

"Tut, tut, I'm afraid that with your chaperone recovering in her room, I'm left to the task, Miss Beauchamps." Her host chuckled.

Richard grasped her hand and brought her fingers to his lips and kissed them, warming them. "This here gal is gonna be my bride soon."

"I am?" She elbowed him. "I don't remember being asked. At least not in person."

James laughed. "I see, well, since a proposal seems to be in order, how about if I settle on the top stair and wait for Mr. Christy to finish his business? Sound fair?"

Without waiting for a response, James removed himself to the stairwell and promptly sat and opened his newspaper.

Richard bent and leaned his forehead against hers.

"Why were you shouting earlier?"

He pressed his mouth near her ear, tickling her with his breath. "So you're fine? He ain't hurt ya or anything?"

She pulled away, and he straightened. "What are you talking about?"

"I'll explain later." Dropping onto one knee, he took her hand in his. "Miss Juliana Beauchamps, if you'll have a lumberjack for a husband, then I won't be in trouble with the Library Board."

Juliana cocked her head. "How is that?"

"When Hatchens' nephew ran off with the newest schoolmarm, leavin' the library high and dry, the Board was right quick to put together a new and better contract for you."

When she pushed a lock of hair from his brow he almost pulled her down into his arms again. "So how are you in trouble?"

"Miss Griffis delivered the contract to the camp by mistake. And me, your Ma, and Claudette—well, we had a nice little bonfire with it that night."

A deep chuckle rose up in her tiny frame. There might be over a foot and a half in height that separated them, but they understood one another. And that counted for a whole lot.

The train, crossing Michigan's Upper Peninsula, rumbled on. Juliana snuggled against her husband's shoulder. With Gracie as her attendant and James as Richard's, they'd been married by Yost's German Lutheran pastor in the church which the Yost family had built near their home. Maisy had wrapped a bouquet of roses, lilies, and Queen Anne's Lace for her. The butler, Rawley, who'd forgiven Richard his brusque treatment, had pinned a rosebud on her groom's new suit coat.

The train whistle announced their next stop, and the train began to slow. Metal screeched against metal and the clack of the wheels turning grew less frantic. Would tonight be as wonderful as those that preceded it?

"You glad I agreed to be your chaperone?" Richard teased as he drew her fingers to his lips, and then kissed them.

Pretending shock, she pulled her hand free and pressed both to her cheeks. "Why, sir, if this is your notion of chaperoning…"

Richard captured her mouth with his and then pulled away. "I love you, Mrs. Christy."

"Mrs. Bon Jean sounds better."

He chuckled, the sound beginning low and rumbling through his broad chest. "How about I call ya that in private?" Richard kissed her cheek and she sighed.

"What are our families going to say?" Juliana whispered as he leaned in and pressed his forehead against hers.

Pulling away, Richard pointed out the window to a bright white three story hotel. "I reckon they'll be right happy that we got hitched, when ya have our son."

"Our daughter, you mean." She poked him in the middle of his chest. "And there are no babies coming our way."

"Yet." He grinned. "But I'm praying God will bless us with a passel of them."

Her heart skipped a beat as his dark eyes pierced hers with meaning. Bon Jean may not have brought her brothers home, but Richard could give her children. "If we have sons, I'd like to name them in honor of my lost brothers. Gerard, Pierre, Phillip were killed in that horrible war and Pascal died in the iron ore mines. Would that be all right with you?"

Richard's eyes widened, and then he tilted his head back and laughed. "You already have four sons planned? I knew there was a good reason we should get married right away. We've got to get started on giving your Ma more grandbabies to spoil."

Her mother wasn't getting any younger. Yet now she was working in a lumber camp. And enjoying it. God sure had surprised them all this past year. "I wish Sean and Connor would come back home from the army. I don't think either has married."

Richard's features tugged in question. "How come they've got Irish names and the others don't?"

"Unlike your family, my mother was the first generation of her family born here and she went by the old ways." Taking a deep breath, Juliana explained the Irish fashion of naming children in a certain order. By the time she was done explaining both the male and female patterns, which were extensive, a groove had formed between her spouse's eyes.

"Maybe we'd best stick with just boys, ya reckon?"

As far as Richard was concerned, they'd flown home on a fancy hot air balloon and not ridden a soot-spouting railroad. Now, though, it was time to come back to earth. And face all the folks back home.

Seated next to him, Juliana squeezed his arm. "Tell me again about Mr. Hatchens. I just can't believe what you said about him."

Richard laughed. "Neither could I. But before I left on the ship, I ran into him. I told him we burned up your contract and he needed to find him a new librarian."

"And you made him squirm, didn't you?" She tapped his arm playfully.

"Reckon so. Let him stew a bit in his own juices before I told him I'd be returnin' from Milwaukee with my bride. Leastwise, I was hopin' you'd be mine." He kissed her forehead.

"And then did he really shake your hand?" Bright blue eyes met his. Would their children have those same Lake Michigan colored eyes or dark ones like his?

"Threw out his hand and pumped mine hard, congratulated me on my good sense. Then acted all sheepish, and said if I'd allow my wife to work until they found a replacement, that he'd be indebted to me."

"Mr. Hatchens must have gagged, having to beg you like that."

"Shucks, no, he gave me a lecture on the Christian way to be a good husband and to cherish my wife and protect her."

"He didn't!" Her pretty mouth formed a perfect O.

"He did. Turns out his own mother ran a boarding house and he believes a woman should be cared for by her husband and stay at home and pampered to the fullest extent possible."

"Pampered at a lumber camp?" It sounded like his sweet wife snorted, but she'd turned her head away.

The conductor walked through. "We'll be in St. Ignace soon."

Checking around them, in their seats and on the floor for anything she'd missed, Juliana placed her bag on her lap. "I've got everything, how about you?"

"Got everything I need right beside me."

Juliana stepped down into her husband's outstretched arms from the train. Nothing in town had changed. But why did it all look brighter? The newly painted buildings, readied for the tourist season, seemed to have been revived just for her. Their vinegar-cleaned windows reflected back the sun's rays as Richard set her down and pulled her toward the area where baggage would be unloaded. How good to be home.

"Moose!" Garrett and Rebecca stood up from a bench near the ferry dock.

Carters carried furniture past them, to a dray parked out on the street. Josephine Christy and her fiancé Tom Jeffries stood by the wagon, watched the men, and pointed to open spots for them to fill. From this vantage point, she couldn't discern what the elaborate designs were, that were carved into the oak chests. A beefy man loaded it with the help of another worker.

"Got a surprise for you, Mrs. Christy." Richard kissed the top of her head.

"I love surprises!"

Rebecca and Garrett joined them and her future sister-in-law drew her into her arms. "We got the telegram. Congratulations, you two!"

Her brother-in-law shook hands with Richard before pulling him into a quick bear hug. "Our baby brother has beat us all to the altar."

Richard pulled away, stretched his shoulders back so that his chest grew even broader and patted there. "And right proud of it, brother. I've got the good sense to recognize an opportunity when I see it and act on it."

Rebecca tugged on Richard's arm. "Did you tell her yet? About your father?"

"I forgot."

Garrett's eyes rolled upward, in apparent disgust, then addressed his comments to Juliana, "Our pa is gonna rent one of your ma's cabins so he can be close to the camp."

"But not too close." Her groom winked at her.

So her mother would have income from the rent. Melanie, Claudette, and her mother would have pay from their cook jobs at the camp. God was answering her prayers. *Thank you, Lord.*

She watched as, without a 'fare thee well', Tom Jeffries and Josephine drove off in the dray.

Garrett jerked a thumb toward the direction in which they'd departed. "We'll meet them out in the camp, but they've got some business to do before we get there."

"Our carriage is over there." Rebecca pointed to a rental from the livery. "You can ride out with us."

"There's our luggage now." Juliana pointed out the banded black leather trunks that James had purchased as a wedding gift.

Garrett patted his stomach. "Jo left us a basket lunch we can eat on the drive out. Reckon we best eat it before we get there and the kids all tear into it."

"Is it in the carriage?" Her husband licked his lips.

With a soft smile, Rebecca gestured to the water. "Frenchie, Pearl, Amelia, and her little brothers and sister went by boat to the Beauchamps with Pa and Irene."

"So they're all out at the camp waitin' on us?"

"Yup."

Had Bell's crew completed the addition to his cabin? Richard's brow began to sweat as they drew closer.

"Are you all right?" Juliana took his hand in his.

"Seems strange having my brother drive."

Rebecca turned and grinned. "I love having him drive me all over Mackinac Island. The children and I have discovered all sorts of fun places to hike and bicycle, but we all love it when Garrett takes us for a ride."

A bump in the road tossed him and Juliana together.

"Oh!" It felt nice having her clutch his arm.

Would she like his gifts? Would there be room? Would he be teased forever? Didn't matter—she was worth it.

As they pulled into the camp, he spied their cottage, now doubled in size, its wood siding much lighter in color than the original building. Pa, hands on hips, watched as the crew lined up.

"What are they doing?" Juliana pointed to the lumberjacks unloading the dray.

Garrett called over his shoulder. "Them shanty boys are settin' up my new gallery."

"Gallery?"

His brother, the talented craftsman, pulled the buggy to a stop. "Sure thing, Juliana. I've made furniture with lilacs burned into the wood, carved into it, or painted on."

His teasing tone must have been lost on Juliana because she frowned and asked, "Why?"

"My baby broth—"

Richard cut him off. "I can't have lilac flowers around me. Makes me sneeze my head off. Shoulda told ya earlier, Juliana."

"Makes him real sick." *Just like Ox to try to have the last word.*

Richard stepped out and secured the horses.

Amy ran from the cook house. "Can we see all the gifts now?"

"Sh!" Rebecca raised her index finger to her mouth.

Helping Juliana out, Richard turned her so he could carry her to the cabin, their new home. "Mr. Christy, put me down."

Her protest was accompanied by giggles, so he ignored it and brought her into the expanded cottage. Fresh lumber scent filled his nostrils. Turning Juliana in a slow half circle, he whispered in her ear. "Do ya see all the lilacs, Juliana?"

"I do." She traced a fingertip over his lips, marveling that this man was her husband, her own Bon Jean. "You must have wanted me here really badly to go to this trouble."

A slow grin covered his handsome face. "And now we have lilacs for you, Juliana, every day of the year."

Tears slipped down her cheeks. No one had ever done something so special for her.

He wrapped his arms around her and pulled her close. "I feel like mailing that Puumala fella a thank you card."

She stiffened. "Oh?" When she tried to pull away, Richard held her fast.

"Yup, he did me a favor and I'm right grateful." He pressed kisses into her hair. "You're the only one for me and that fool man made it possible for me to marry ya. So if I ever do meet him, I'll shake his hand."

Laughter bubbled up out of her. "You're thinking of that right now?"

"I worried about Yost and then I got to worryin' about Puumala and by the time I got to Milwaukee I had a full head of steam on."

"Poor Rawley. He got the brunt of it."

"Yost thanked me for not punching him, when I explained what all we feared. Said I spared his daughter some trauma."

"Isabelle has suffered more than a child that age should. But I think Gracie has done wonders with her. She takes marvelous care of her."

"So do ya think she might stay there?"

"I don't know." She placed her hands on his cheeks. "But I do know where I'm staying—right here with you."

Where God had been leading her all along.

The End

Author's Notes

Railroads continued to make huge inroads to all parts of our great nation, including Michigan's Upper Peninsula. And boat travel on the Great Lakes was a popular way to reach a destination quickly.

As I mentioned in *The Fruitcake Challenge* and *The Lumberjacks' Ball*, I really am the descendant of lumberjacks and I have a cousin who continues to work in the industry. The mighty pines of Michigan drew my ancestors up north. Michigan's Eastern Upper Peninsula was becoming a busy place at the turn of the century. My grandfather ran a lumber camp near my hometown.

In this book, because I gave the matriarch, Nora O'Rourke Beauchamps, an Irish heritage, first generation in America, I had her name her children in the Irish conventions. This resulted in the alternating of French names, from the father's side, and Irish names from the mother's side (from Irish Genealogy Toolkit website).

A great many men died in the Civil War. The statistics are different between the North and South, with more Southern families having experienced a loss. One demographic, I read, was one in four dead from the North. Three of the four fictional Beauchamps sons fighting in the war died, an unusually large loss.

St. Ignace, Michigan, was a busy city at the turn of the century, with four newspapers and a vibrant tourist industry. Today, it is a small town in Michigan's Upper Peninsula, but still lovely. You can download a walking tour PDF from the Fort DeBuade website (www.fortdebuade.com) to give you an idea of St. Ignace's street layout. (Click here from a tablet for the walking tour pdf.)

By the turn of the century, lumberjacks had harvested most of Lower Michigan's "White Gold"—virgin white pines that could be as big around as a man was tall. The camps moved on to the Upper Peninsula, where hardwoods were more predominant, as well as the pines.

The Paul Bunyan stories that we know today originally derived from Paul Bon Jean folklore. These tales were told for decades, in the lumber camps, before someone finally put the stories into print. Lumberjacks lived an isolated life, as far as social amenities, and often amused each other with tall tales. Bon Jean stories resulted in a far "bigger than life" lumberjack but were a representation of the camp culture. I grew up with the whole Paul Bunyan lore around me. We even had a Paul Bunyan restaurant in my hometown of Newberry, Michigan!

Lilacs are abundant in northern Michigan (Lower Peninsula), and in the Upper Peninsula, but especially on Mackinac Island, where many varieties flourish and an annual Lilac Festival is held. The lilacs were brought to the area by French settlers. The area has a rich French history and the French military occupied the area until after the French Indian Wars ended. So there are families with French names, whose ancestors may have lived in the area for over four hundred years.

Although most librarians today are female, in times past male librarians were the norm, especially before the turn of the 20th century. But women were attending "normal schools" or colleges, especially in progressive states of Michigan and Ohio. The Dewey Decimal System (or Classification) was rather new in the 1890s and most librarians hadn't been trained in the method, which was still somewhat controversial. Something we take for granted, as far as bringing order in our library searches, was only just coming into full acceptance during this time.

Thank you for reading Book Three in The Christy Lumber Camp Series! If you enjoyed reading Lilacs for Juliana, would you please consider posting a review on Amazon, goodreads, or another social media review site?

Acknowledgements

First I want to thank my Heavenly Father; every book is for you! Thank you to my husband, Jeffrey, and my son, Clark, for bearing with me as I wrote this book and my daughter, Cassandra, for her input.

I raise my teacup to thank Debbie Lynn Costello for help as a wonderful critique partner. Thank you to my Pagels Pals Readers and Reviewers Group on Facebook—such a blessing to me! You keep me going!

And more toasts go out to my Beta readers: Sonja Hoeke Nishimoto, Regina Fujitani, Tina St. Clair Rice, Gracie Yost (thanks for letting me "borrow" your names, too!). Many thanks to advance readers: Robin Bunting, Deanna Stevens, Betti Mace, Ann Ellison, Angi Griffis, Cheryl Baranski, Nancy McLeroy, Britney Adams, Chicki Crawford Foley, Chris Granville and Anne Payne. Thanks to my advance readers the Overcoming with God blogger "Angels": Diana Flowers, Teresa Mathews, Noela Nancarrow, and Bonnie Roof.

Thank you to Narielle Living for editing this novel. Any errors in the book are my own. Thank you, Cynthia Hickey, for my cover—Juliana and her lilacs came to life! Thank you to Amber Goos, my cover model who makes a lovely Juliana, and to Reginia Fujitani and Kathleen Harwell for arranging the photo shoot.

I'd like to acknowledge the librarians at the York County Library for their suggestions, which were invaluable, and for supporting local authors. In particular I want to thank Eric Wilson, Library Assistant, from Hampton, Virginia, for discussing early library science with me and giving me suggested reading.

Thank you, also, to the folks at the Tahquamenon Logging Museum in Newberry, Michigan.

Author Biography

<u>Carrie Fancett Pagels</u> "Hearts Overcoming Through Time" is an award-winning and Amazon best-selling Christian historical fiction author. Carrie enjoys reading, traveling, baking, and beading—but not all at the same time! Many of her stories are set in Michigan, where she grew up. Possessed with an overactive imagination, she loves sharing her stories with others. A psychologist for twenty-five years, she is no longer practicing. Married for twenty-eight years to the man of her dreams, with a teenage son and adult daughter. Carrie resides in Virginia's Historic Triangle, which is perfect for her fascination with history. Under contract with White Rose/Pelican Book Group, Forget-Me-Not Press, and Barbour Publishing.

<u>Contact Information:</u> Websites: CarrieFancettPagels.com, OvercomingWithGod.com, and ColonialQuills.org
Carrie is on Facebook, Twitter, goodreads (cfpagels), pinterest, LinkedIn, and Google+.

OTHER BOOKS BY CARRIE FANCETT PAGELS

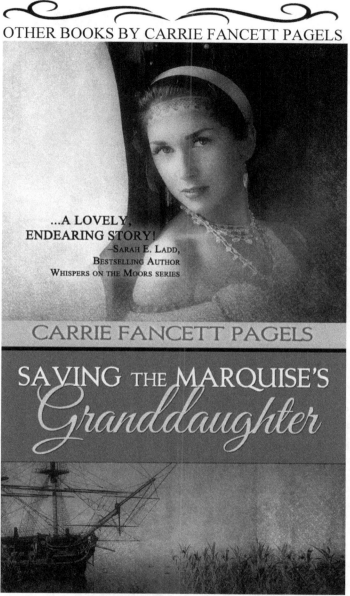

A young French aristocrat must flee her homeland when her family is discovered to be Huguenots. Can a German peasant save her? And at what cost? Available from White Rose/Pelican Books in June 2016.

Carrie's novella, "Requilted with Love", set at the Michigan State Fair in 1889, is one of fine historical romances set at American State Fairs. Will a quilter who has lost two loves risk her heart on a a balloonist? Available from Barbour Books in November, 2016. .

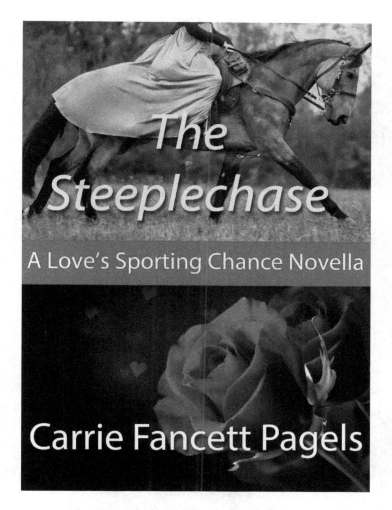

It's 1810 in Williamsburg, Virginia, and when a young woman finds her family threatened she takes matters into her own hands – risking her life in a race to the steeple. From Forget Me Not Romances (February, 2016).

A young seamstress, in obedience to God, remains at a place that puts her at great risk. But will a thespian, forced into Confederate service, rescue her? Re-released under new cover, Return to Shirley Plantation – A Civil War Romance (January, 2016) was Carrie's debut in Christian fiction in 2013!

The Substitute Bride (Hearts Overcoming Press, October, 2015)

"It's A Wonderful Life" meets "A Christmas Carol"

A letter for Sonja's deceased friend arrives at the post office in Michigan, and with it a proposal. With her father threatening to kick her out of his home, Sonja impulsively responds, offering to travel west to be a substitute bride. At the same time, Louis's railroad promotion sends him back to Michigan, the one place on earth he'd hoped to never return—where Christmas past was full of pain. A mysterious stranger leaves him marked copies of "A Christmas Carol" as he considers romancing Sonja in Christmas present. Will Louis discern the best choices for Christmas future? Does it include the Poor House, again? Love? Or both?

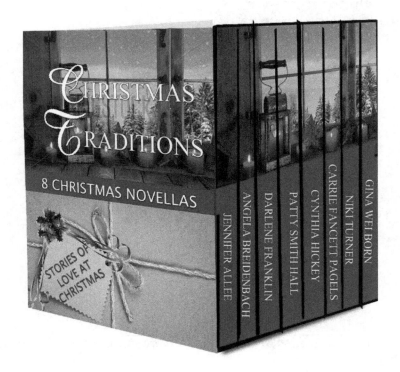

Contributor to: <u>Christmas Traditions Eight-in-One</u> Boxed set (Forget-Me-Not Press, July 2015) is available on Amazon in Kindle format.

Eight heart-warming Christian novellas, including Carrie Fancett Pagels' *The Fruitcake Challenge*!

A feisty camp cook accepts a handsome lumberjack's challenge to make a fruitcake as good as his mother made—and he'll marry her! The Fruitcake Challenge novella is the first book in The Christy Lumber Camp series and a Selah Award Finalist. With endorsements from Serena B. Miller, Julie Lessman, MaryLu Tyndall, and more. Selah Award finalist and Family Fiction Book of the Year finalist.

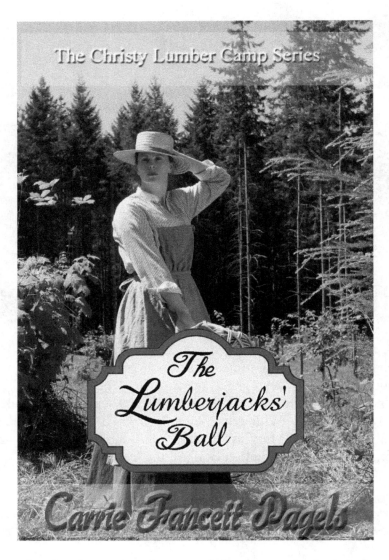

Can the lumberjack who saved her once before help a mercantile owner overcome her past? The Lumberjacks' Ball is a short novel and Book Two in The Christy Lumber Camp Series (Hearts Overcoming Press, 2015) available in ebook and print.

Carrie's 1940's short story, "Snowed In," is published in Volume One, Tales of Faith and Family for the Holidays in Guidepost Books (2013) *A Cup of Christmas Cheer*.

CPSIA information can be obtained
at www.ICGtesting.com
Printed in the USA
LVHW05s2316240718
584848LV00009B/237/P